A MYSTERY BEFORE CHRISTMAS

ADRIANA LICIO

The HomeTravellers
Press

A Mystery Before Christmas

Book 3 in the *An Italian Village Mystery* series
By Adriana Licio

Edition I
Copyright 2019 © Adriana Licio
ISBN: 978-88-32249-02-6

Cover by Wicked Smart Design
Editing by Alison Jack

To Valentino,
Christmases are a piece of magic

CONTENTS

1 DECEMBER - A STEAMY CLAYPOT

"Mum, isn't this place the most beautiful in the world?" said young Betta, looking at the Maratea gulf from the bench on which she was sitting with her mother.

"Indeed it is."

"They have the mountains, they have the sea, can't we stay and live here?"

"I'm afraid we can't, young lady. I'd say it's time to move on to Naples."

"Oh, Mum, just another ten minutes. Look at the little houses over there. Wouldn't it be a dream to own one?"

"We'd better go, Betta, but I promise we will come back. You know, from Naples all we have to do is jump on a train to visit Maratea any time we want. And we will have Capri and Ischia nearby, and Sorrento. You'll love it there too."

But Anna didn't believe what she was saying herself. Like her daughter, she wished she could live in a quiet little village by the sea, but she needed to find a job. The opportunities the big city offered would allow her to earn enough to live a simple but decent life. That's what she hoped, at least. Life without Alex hadn't been easy so far.

"Come on, let's go." Anna took hold of Betta's hand and they headed towards the car. But when she climbed into the driver's seat and started the engine, it gave a feeble little murmur and died.

"What's wrong with it now?" Anna tried again, two, three times, but the engine's murmur was getting more feeble with each attempt until it ceased completely. The car simply wouldn't start.

Just what I need! Anna thought, trying to quell her rising anguish.

A woman she and Betta had exchanged a few words with in the central square stopped by to enquire if they needed help.

"Oh, thank you for asking, my car won't start. Do you know where I can find a garage?"

The woman shook her head. "It's Saturday afternoon, I'm afraid you'll have to wait until Monday."

"Monday!" Anna shrieked in horror. "Maybe it's only the battery. If someone would just help me to get it started, we'll be on our way to Naples."

The woman didn't look convinced. "I don't know much about cars, but if there's a problem, I'd say you'd better wait for it to be fixed. Imagine if you were to break down on the highway – it would be far more expensive to be picked up and towed away from there."

Expensive? How I loathe the very word. Anna's dark brown eyes opened wide in dismay, making her little face look even smaller and paler than usual.

"You'll need a place for the night," said the woman, as if reading Anna's mind. "I rent a small flat out to tourists in the high season, but at this time of year things are quiet, so I will only charge you for the heating and linen." She said her price and Anna breathed again; in Naples, accommodation would have cost so much more.

"Let's fetch your bags from the boot, it's just a short walk from here. I will ask my husband to call Nico, the mechanic, and see if he can have a look at your car. He may be able to do it tomorrow, but it's more likely to be on Monday."

"That's so very kind of you." But Anna felt embarrassed at being completely dependent on a stranger's kindness.

"Are we really sleeping here?" Betta asked the woman.

"You are. Do you like this town?"

"I love it!" Betta replied, a wide grin crossing her freckled face.

"My name is Nennella, by the way, and I own the newsstand on the other side of the town."

Betta and Anna introduced themselves and fetched their bags from the car. The apartment was in a little cobbled alley. It was cold inside, but Nennella switched on the heaters as soon as they were through the door.

"It will get very warm in a couple of hours," she said, showing them around. Then, looking more closely at Betta, she added, "This young one has very shiny eyes. You've not got a fever, have you?" She pressed her cheek against Betta's forehead, and then turned to Anna. "You'd better put her to bed."

Anna looked at her daughter; the woman was right. Betta had burning cheeks and bright, watery eyes.

"Oh, Betta, how do you feel?"

"I'm fine, Mum, I really am. I'm so happy we're staying here for the night."

"I'll fetch you a hot water bottle," said Nennella. "I live not far from here. In the meantime, make yourself comfortable."

After showing them where the towels and linen were, she left the young mother and feverish little girl alone.

∿

BETTA WAS SLEEPING, BREATHING HEAVILY AS SHE DID WHEN SHE was sick. Anna had made up the beds, unpacked their things from their bags, and now she was sitting next to a heater to warm up a little, feeling helpless. She had left Aunt Battistina's home in Calabria; her aunt was the last living relative she had. And now here she was, stuck in the middle of nowhere. Was she mad?

The whole plan had been plain stupid; the most sensible thing to do would be to go back to her aunt. At the thought, though, Anna pushed her head against Betta's blankets and burst into silent tears, clenching her teeth to hold back her sobs so she wouldn't wake up her daughter.

She needed to buy some food, but she doubted the shops would still be open. She'd have to ask at a restaurant for a takeaway. As the practicalities filled her mind, she wiped her tears away.

The doorbell rang. Roundish and bubbly, Nennella came in, followed by Biagio, her quiet, lanky husband. He held a steaming red claypot in his hands while his wife did all the talking.

"This is a wholesome soup for you two. It will keep you warm and help your daughter recover too. And here is some bread and cheese and everything else you might need for tomorrow's breakfast." She moved into the kitchen, putting stuff in the fridge, the fruit basket, the bread box. "This is Doctor Tramutola's phone number, he is very good with kids. I told him you might need his services should Betta's temperature rise. He is old school and will come to see her tomorrow morning, if you need him to. Just call him early."

Anna felt so grateful, she was unable to speak. Stunned silence was actually the way most people reacted to Nennella's incessant chatter, but Anna wasn't to know that.

"I think you're all settled." Nennella touched Betta's

forehead gently and added, "You shouldn't leave tomorrow, even if Nico can fix the car. This little one has a nasty fever."

Anna finally managed to get a word in edgeways. "Do you think we might stay here for one more night?"

"Not many tourists until we get closer to Christmas, so you can stay as long as you want, dear. But we'd better go, you look like you need a good rest too. I'll pop in tomorrow, and here's some paracetamol for Betta."

Biagio muttered something about the car and Anna handed him her keys. When the couple left, she felt like two angels had just passed by, leaving behind a heart-warming welcome and a red claypot from which the most delicious smell was coming.

2 DECEMBER – A ROBIN

"Nooooo!" A sharp cry resonated around the house. "Fernando, Fernando, come in here. Please!"

Mr Orlando joined his wife. "What has happened?"

"My pendant has gone!" his wife cried, showing him the empty case.

"Maybe you put it somewhere else last night," he said, doing his best to disguise his fear. The woman showed him the broken window pane.

"Someone broke in! They stole it!"

"Oh my goodness, how could they have known exactly how to get in?" Mr Orlando went outside. The little balcony could be reached by dropping down from the solid guttering. It wasn't an easy manoeuvre, but it wasn't impossible either. "We'd better call the carabinieri."

THE DOORBELL RANG.

"Good morning, I'm just calling in to make sure you're fine and you've got all you need," Nennella said.

"Please, come in," Anna replied. As Nennella accepted the invitation and followed her into the small but sparklingly clean living room, she added, "The doctor came early this morning. I decided to call him even though she's only got a slight fever now, just to be on the safe side."

"You're right, better safe than sorry. And Dr Tramutola is such a comfort, isn't he?" Nennella said, sitting down on a chair next to the table, her eyes inspecting the spotless crystal chandelier above her head. Not one single grain of dust was allowed to settle in her presence.

"Indeed, he is a good man," Anna replied. She couldn't help following Nennella's gaze up to the ceiling as she continued speaking. "He approved the dose of paracetamol, but he says there's nothing to worry about. Just a cold with a bit of a fever, and if the fever has come down tomorrow, she can go out as normal the day after."

"I'm pleased to hear that. Kids can go from feverish to healthy in a couple of days, can't they? I'm just glad my flat was empty so I could help you out. Now you won't mind me doing this," she said, putting a newspaper on the sturdy wooden chair where she had been sitting, and climbing on top of it. A handkerchief in her hand, she polished the chandelier's three crystal flowers, each one holding a lightbulb, until they shone, chirping away merrily the whole time as if she were sitting comfortably on the sofa. "Also, the mechanic has taken a look at your car. It would seem the battery is rather old and needs to be replaced, but as it's Sunday, he can't get a new one until tomorrow. You wouldn't have gone far in that car."

"Oh, I don't know how to thank you…"

"No need for that. But I have to admit, I am a nosey lady," she said, landing on the floor, removing the newspaper from the chair and finally sitting down. "Would it be very rude if I were to ask you if you're all alone?"

"Of course not." Anna gave a look towards the bedroom; Betta was sound asleep. "Yes, we are alone. Alex, my husband, passed away two years ago. We lived in Milan at the time. After his death, I tried to make ends meet, but the cost of living is rather high there."

"Did you have a job? And how did you manage with Betta?"

"Yes, I had a job at the reception of a private clinic. It paid enough to keep the two of us going. Also, I had a kind neighbour who helped me, watching Betta when I was at work. But she fell sick and had to go into a home for the elderly, and I wasn't earning enough to pay for a childminder too. Betta is a very responsible child, but she's too young to be left alone all day. I have one relative, an aunt on my mother's side, who lives in Calabria. She invited us to stay with her, and I knew life would be cheaper down south." Anna stopped.

"And have you now left her home?" Nennella asked without missing a beat.

Anna sighed. "It might sound rather ungrateful, but I didn't like life there. Aunt Battistina is a strong character and she wanted to control our lives entirely. Even if I was using my own money, she'd complain we were living on her charity. Also, I couldn't find any kind of work for myself, while Auntie was far too harsh with Betta."

Anna didn't mention how mean Aunt Battistina had been towards her too, nor did she refer to the woman's strict religious doctrines and the absurd rules she'd imposed on mum and daughter.

"It couldn't last. Though, in all truth, right now I'm not sure I've made the wisest choice. I hope I'll find a job in Naples, and a way to keep Betta safe when she's not at school."

"Well, in all honesty, I don't think going to Naples on your own, without knowing anyone there, is a great idea. But we will sort something out. One of the reasons I popped by was to ask if you want me to look after Betta, in case you need to go out for a while."

"I do want to buy something for lunch and dinner, so that would be very kind of you."

"The small mini-market in the main square is open in the mornings on a Sunday, and there's a trattoria at the end of this alley if you want to fetch a takeaway. Off you go, now."

~

It was late afternoon when Giò Brando entered her sister's perfumery. She looked around, her green eyes showing her disappointment.

"At least you have a few Christmas things out. But there's nothing in the village at all. That's a shame!"

"But it's the tradition here, you know that," Agnese reminded her sister. "Christmas officially starts on the eighth of December."

The two women couldn't have looked more different. Agnese's face was a perfect oval with distinctively Mediterranean features and intense dark eyes. Her slightly plump figure was smartly dressed in skirt and blouse. Giò, on the other hand, was tall with short dark hair, her boyish figure sporting jeans, fitted jacket and a colourful scarf.

"But that's too late! The festivities will be over before they've even started." Giò was spending her first Christmas in her hometown after having lived in the UK for a number of years. She had broken up with her fiancé just before the wedding was due to take place and decided to go back home after having spent a decade in London, trying to keep him happy. Dorian Gravy had always hated Maratea so she had given up spending Christmases at home. Deep in her heart, she had always missed them, but now she felt disappointed. In the UK, the Christmas season would have started just after Halloween. On the streets of Maratea, it was now December and there were still no Christmas lights, no Christmas trees, and only a handful of shops displaying cheerful seasonal decorations.

"Well, I try to get started on the first December in the shop," Agnese said, pointing to the windows which were festooned with red ribbons and felt decorations.

"But it's Sunday, your shop is open and there's virtually no one around."

"The first Sunday of the month is always like that, but it's fine by me. I have so much work to do." Agnese pointed to a number of boxes next to the counter, "I don't mind having a little time to prepare it all."

"I don't know – the weather is warm, the sun is shining. It doesn't look like Christmas at all."

"How's your writing going?" asked Agnese, suspecting her sister's blue mood was due more to personal reasons than a lack of decorations in the streets.

"I've done my first draft and I'm starting the edits," Giò answered, waving her hand as if dismissing a nightmare. "I thought I'd celebrate with a Christmas walk…"

"Sorry, but you'll have to wait." Agnese chuckled before adding, "And at home, Granny won't allow you to get the Christmas tree up until the eighth of December, as tradition dictates."

"I'm planning on buying one for my flat, just a little one, but I'm not sure I will find it today. It seems as though everyone in Maratea is determined to ignore the fact that it's Christmas."

"The good news is that this year, to allow businesses to enjoy a full working day on the eighth of December, Mayor Zucchini has decided the Christmas lights will be turned on on the evening of the seventh, in time for the official start of the festivities." With a grin, Agnese added, "You're getting an extra half day of Christmas."

But Giò just shrugged and left her sister's perfumery. She needed a walk, decorations or no decorations. Editing was tough for her; it required attention to all manner of minutiae, something her temperamental nature wasn't too keen on. She walked to the Villa Comunale, the public garden almost at the end of the village, and there sat on a bench. As it was nearly dark, the yellow lamps were on. The damp of the grass and the trees made her shiver a bit; this was the closest she'd get to a Christmas atmosphere for the day.

A little robin stood on the branches above her head. He was bobbing up and down, indifferent to the encroaching darkness, giving out a little chirp every now and then.

"Aren't you out a bit late? Anyway, I'm glad you're enjoying yourself."

Giò rested her head against a tree trunk, breathing in the light scent of damp moss. She closed her eyes and imagined a traditional Christmas scene with snow, kids singing, streets shining with lights, a Christmas Market and the scent of mulled wine in the air.

"*The carillon!*" murmured a voice.

Giò's eyes flew open and she looked around, startled. There was nobody in view. The little bird bowed his head and disappeared up to the higher branches, maybe to his nest.

Who spoke? Did I dream it? Giò wondered. *Carillon* – it was ages since she'd last heard that word, used in Italy to refer to any sort of musical box. *Time to go home. Never mind Christmas lights, it looks like I'm getting Christmas hallucinations.*

3 DECEMBER – A MISSING BOOK

Agnese was opening the boxes the courier had just delivered, containing a collection of candles she had ordered in for Christmas. They were no ordinary candles; they were of the finest quality, made from six different types of beeswax. This would allow them to burn slowly, and as they warmed up, they would release the perfume they contained. No commercial fragrance, this was a real perfume composed by a true perfume master – first the head or starting notes, then the middle or heart ones, and finally the back notes. A heart-warming tale coming to life under your very nose. The candles had not been cheap and Agnese hoped her customers would appreciate their beauty, including the stunning handmade ceramic pots they sat in.

The doorbell rang as Nennella came in. The chatty woman actually stopped on the threshold to read the notice Agnese had posted on her door.

'Christmas help needed.'

She then smiled. "Good morning, Agnese."

"Good morning, Nennella. Please do come in."

"I'm glad to see this," the older woman indicated the

notice. Then looking around, she added, "I imagine you've not found anybody yet."

"Exactly, each year it seems to get more difficult."

"How about Giò, can't she help you?"

"She will in the last-minute rush up to Christmas... but she has work to finish by early January, and I need full-time help." Agnese showed Nennella the number of boxes she had waiting to be opened, all full of items needing to be checked, inventoried and priced, their details inserted onto the sales software.

"Well, I might have the right person for you," and Nennella told her about Anna.

"Poor souls. Such a sad story, but wouldn't it be better for them to go on to Naples as soon as they can so the little girl can get started in school?"

"Big city, I guess she won't be allowed to start in a new school until after the Christmas holidays. In Maratea, she can start tomorrow – I've already spoken to the teachers. Also, at Christmas, a lot of people return here from Naples to visit family. They might be able to help Anna find a cheap flat, not to mention a job."

"And you think she might be willing to help me in the shop?"

"She'd love that. She is a sensible, trustworthy young woman, she's longing to work, and I believe... she's your type."

Agnese laughed at that. "I didn't know I had a type."

"Well, there's something different about this shop of yours. It's never been like any other in town. You're very practical in some respects, but it's clear this is more than just a business for you. Anna, for some reason, seems to be cut from the same cloth as you. Would you like to meet her?"

"Of course. Tell her to come in this afternoon, before opening time."

∽

ANNA ENTERED PIAZZA VITOLO, THE SQUARE IN FRONT OF Maratea Town Hall, and looked around to find the alley on the right-hand side that Nennella had mentioned. Spotting a sign displaying the perfumery name, she walked in that direction and stopped in front of windows framed in turquoise wood. Peering curiously through the windows and liking what she saw, she moved towards the door and saw the notice.

It was the right place.

A nice smell of smoky wood, pine needles and sage welcomed her as she walked through the door, looking around.

"Hello, can I help you?" Agnese said.

"Good morning, Mrs Fiorillo, I'm Anna Giordano. Nennella told me I could come to have a chat with you." But as she spoke, Anna's eyes continued to wander around. She couldn't help herself – the place was beyond fantastic. She had imagined a modern perfumery, but this was something totally different.

White and turquoise cabinets and old bookcases displayed perfume bottles and toiletries. A vintage letterpress on the wall was filled with soaps from Portugal in vibrant colours, while in the centre of the room, an ebony table displayed gift sets especially for Christmas along with candles and, at its feet, beautiful white lanterns from Sweden, pillows with snowflake designs and fleece blankets patterned with forest creatures.

"This is beautiful," Anna said with such simplicity, Agnese had no doubt she was sincere.

"Glad you like it." Then, seeing Anna sniffing the air and looking around again, Agnese added, "And no, there's no fireplace. It's just that winter candle giving off the scent of burned wood and pine needles."

"It feels so cosy!" Anna smiled. "I really thought there must be a fireplace somewhere." She paused, as if to remind herself she was not there to shop. "Maybe I'm chatting too much. I came because Nennella told me you are looking for a sales assistant for the Christmas season."

"Have you any experience of working in a shop?"

"I'm afraid not, but I am willing to learn." Anna looked up at the boxes near the computer, then at Agnese entering the items one by one into the sales software. "And I'm quite good with computer stuff."

"Oooh, I'd love a hand with this. It's the part I struggle with most."

"If you just show me how to do it once, I'll be glad to help."

"That will be very useful. Over the next few days, we will need to get ready for the rush. After the eighth of December, we'll mostly be concentrating on sales and gift wrapping."

"I did a course on paper craft, so I might be able to help with that as well. But I'm afraid I'm not familiar with perfumes and creams and make-up."

"Nor were the helpers I got in for Christmas in the past." Agnese smiled. "Let's start by sorting out that stuff near the counter. Do you think you can spare an hour to work with me now?"

"I certainly can. But I do have a young daughter. I don't know how, but Nennella convinced the school to let her join classes from tomorrow. In the afternoons, would you mind if she stayed here with me during working hours? She's very quiet."

"I've got a daughter too, about the same age I believe. Lilia is eight."

"Betta turned eight in August."

"They could do their homework together in the afternoons. My grandma will watch over them."

"That'd be perfect." Anna smiled, knowing how much Betta would love to have a new friend – particularly a friend in Maratea.

Agnese showed Anna how the software worked. The young woman learned fast and fed the details of all the new candles and gift sets into the system far more quickly than Agnese could have managed it. As Nennella had guessed, Anna was an uncomplicated but efficient soul.

"I think we can stop here for today since you've left your little girl with Nennella," Agnese said, going on to inform Anna about pay and working hours. Anna replied she had no need to think it over – she was glad to accept the job offer and start work the next morning.

"MRS LIBRETTO, I CAN'T FIND MATILDA, THE BOOK YOU READ TO us last Saturday. Did someone borrow it?" Luca asked, his dark eyes extremely serious.

Laura Libretto, Maratea's librarian, smiled at the boy in front of her. "I don't think so," she said, checking on the computer. "The book should be here. Maybe someone just put it back in the wrong place."

They went through the books on the returns trolley together, then looked on the children's shelves of the library. Mrs Libretto checked the more popular adult sections, just in case a distracted father or mother had dropped it there while searching for their own favourite books. Nothing.

"It seems it's not here, but I'm sure it will pop up when I sort out the other books. Some readers are rather careless. I'll drop it off at your mother's shop if it turns up. In the meantime, why don't you read *Charlie and the Chocolate Factory*?"

"I loved Matilda's superpowers, but I will give this a go," Luca said, taking the book she was handing to him and going to sit in the reading room.

Mrs Libretto watched him sit down and start reading quietly next to Tommaso, an older man who was fond of philosophy. As for herself – well, in all honesty, she was rather worried. *Matilda* wasn't the first book to have gone missing from the library in the last few weeks.

4 DECEMBER – A STARTLING RESEMBLANCE

"Good afternoon, madam, is there anything I can do for you?" Anna asked politely. An older lady, her slight figure dressed all in black, had just entered the shop.

"Yes, dear, I'm looking for ideas. Christmas is coming, and though I'm not fond of buying presents, there are a few people I can't neglect."

Anna asked what kind of presents she was looking for, and then they started to go through the numerous options the shop offered for the festive season.

"Isn't Agnese in today?"

"She's just gone to run a quick errand, she should be back any minute. Do you want me to call her?"

"No, not at all. You're very helpful too, it's just strange not to see her."

"She'll be back soon."

The door opened and Lilia and Betta came in. Lilia, as self-confident as ever, came forward and spoke to the customer.

"Good afternoon, Mrs De Blasi."

"Hello, Lilia, you're growing up fast. I almost didn't recognise you."

Lilia swelled with pride.

"Are you with a friend?" Mrs De Blasi indicated Betta, who was lingering at the entrance.

"This is my daughter," Anna said, calling Betta forward. "Betta, come over to say hello."

As the child came forward, Mrs De Blasi froze. The green eyes under a fringe of dark blonde hair; the little nose and the curve of the mouth; even the scattering of freckles across Betta's face. The older woman staggered and Anna had to catch her and help her to sit down on a nearby seat.

At that moment, the doorbell tinkled and Agnese came in, surprised to find two scared girls, a woman fainting on one of her armchairs, and Anna looking beyond relieved to see her.

"Please, Agnese, get Mrs De Blasi a glass of water with two spoonfuls of sugar."

When she had drunk the sugary water down, some colour returned to Mrs De Blasi's face. "I'm so sorry," she murmured.

"How do you feel? Do you want me to call a doctor?"

"No, not at all. I'm feeling better now." She searched the room with her eyes, stopping only when they lighted upon Betta. "Would you remind this silly old lady what your name is?"

"Elisabetta," Betta stuttered, feeling rather self-conscious as the attention of everyone present was on her.

"Oh my goodness!" Mrs De Blasi went rigid, looking even paler than she had when she'd felt faint. Agnese and Anna looked at each other in confusion. What was going on here?

The old woman swallowed. After an awkward pause, she spoke to Betta again.

"How old are you?"

Now Betta was too shy to speak. The woman's eyes were piercing right through her.

"She is eight years old," Anna replied for her daughter.

"Then it can't be. How stupid of me. I'm sorry, forgive this old lady. My son passed away 13 years ago, but foolishly, I still find myself searching for him in the faces of people I meet." Mrs De Blasi smiled the saddest smile Agnese had ever seen. "My Marco had the same beautiful eyes as yours, Betta."

"I'm told I look like my father," Betta said. Now that the tension had dissipated somewhat, she had found her tongue again. "But his name was Alex."

"Then Alex must be a very handsome dad."

"He was," Anna said. "But like your son, he passed away far too soon, two years ago. Do you have any grandsons or granddaughters?"

"Unfortunately not. But I don't want to sadden you all with old stories, nor evoke painful memories. I will return another day to buy my presents. Now, I'd prefer to go home."

"I will accompany you," Anna said promptly. "If that's OK with you, Agnese?"

"Of course, I would have suggested you do that anyway."

"I wish I could say not to worry, but I'm still a bit shaken, so I would really appreciate it."

"Betta, you wait for me here. It's your first day out since you were ill, so you need to be careful."

Betta nodded obediently, but Lilia said, "We need to go back home. We have tons of homework, but between the two of us, we will soon get it done."

"OK, but please, no more going outside, at least for today."

Anna offered her arm to the older woman and they left for Mrs De Blasi's home, chatting on the way with the instant camaraderie that only two people who have experienced intense grief can have.

～

"Granny, is Auntie Adelina coming on Thursday?" Lilia asked that evening at dinner.

"Yes, she's finally coming. I can't wait to see her, and she's staying until New Year. I'm so glad..."

"Until you start quarrelling," Luca said wryly.

Agnese gave him a stern look, but Giò and Lilia chuckled.

"It's only normal to argue every now and then with my beloved sister," Gran explained.

"How did it go with Betta?" Agnese asked Lilia.

"She's going to be my best friend. Along with Giorgia, I mean."

"She's a very sweet child," added Granny. "How about her mother? Will she be a help to you, Agnese?"

"Indeed she will. She picks everything up so quickly, and I never thought it could be such fun to work with someone else in the shop. I usually only hire staff for the Christmas and summer seasons out of necessity, but Anna is both pleasant and efficient, so I might end up missing her when she leaves. I hope it won't be too tiring for her, though. After all, she's all alone with a child to look after."

"It will be harder when she gets to Naples," Giò said. "She won't work a few hundred metres from home then, so I'm not too sure how she will cope with the child and all."

Agnese nodded. "Nennella is helping Anna find some sort of association in Naples that helps single mothers organise care for their children at a reasonable price."

"That would be good," Granny said, nodding in approval. "And I guess Maratea folks who live in Naples will be back for the holidays and might help her to find a house."

"There will be no Nennella's rates in Naples, though," Giò said.

"It won't be an easy start," Granny agreed. "Maybe we could help her with a little extra cash. How about asking the

Pink Slippers Society to raise some money for her via the Christmas Market?"

"They were meant to donate to some big charity this year," Agnese thought aloud, "but it'd make more sense to help someone who's closer to us."

Granny said she would speak to Ornella Capello, the President of the Pink Slippers Society and a former pupil of hers. The society usually ran a kiosk or two at the Christmas Market, selling cakes or arts and crafts made by the members to raise money for a good cause.

Lilia jumped up. "This year, the good cause will be Betta and her mum," she shouted in delight.

5 DECEMBER – THE PINK SLIPPERS

B etta and Lilia had finished their homework. Unusually, it was Giò supervising them as Granny had gone to visit a neighbour.

The Brandos lived in the same building housing three independent flats. Granny lived on the ground floor, and would be sharing her flat with Auntie Adelina for the Christmas holidays. On the first floor were Agnese and her family, and in the smaller attic lived Giò. In Granny's flat under Giò's guidance, the two girls had finished their homework in double quick time, which was *not* because – as Agnese would have insinuated – Giò had helped them too much, doing the homework herself to get the job done. Patience was not one of Giò's virtues.

Whatever the case, the homework was finished and the two girls were playing games by the time Anna arrived at Granny's flat to fetch her daughter. Giò and she had hardly exchanged a few words before Giò's attention was grabbed by Betta singing.

"Where did you learn that tune?"

"I just know it."

"Maybe at school?"

"No, not really. It's just in my head."

"It is an old Christmas song from Scotland," Giò remarked. "I doubt many kids in Southern Italy would know it."

"Actually, her father used to sing it all the time at Christmas. I don't know where he learned it, but I guess it's stayed in Betta's memory."

"Really, Mum, was it Dad's song?"

"Yes, his Christmas favourite."

Betta swelled with pride; she loved anything to do with her father, like when her mum said she had his eyes and looked at her with such tenderness.

"She certainly wouldn't have picked it up in Maratea, I've never heard that tune here," Giò said. "But guess what? Now it makes me homesick for the UK. When I was there, I missed Christmas with my family. And now I miss that very special British atmosphere."

"Would you like to be back there?"

"That's a good question. The ideal would be to spend a few days there, say hello to old friends, tour the English countryside, return to bonnie Scotland to visit Glasgow and Edinburgh and see them all dressed up for Christmas, and then come back here. I guess we travellers are never happy with what we've got." Giò laughed, flushing a bit as she did every time she felt she was wanting too much from life.

"I'm so happy to be here," Anna whispered. "I would never have dreamed we'd have the promise of such a beautiful Christmas."

"I told you, Mum, I love it here too," Betta piped up. "I don't think we should go to Naples at all."

"As we agreed, we will just live in the here and now and enjoy what we have wholeheartedly." Anna was determined not to let her fear of an uncertain future spoil the pleasure of the present time.

At that moment, Granny and Agnese returned. When Anna announced she and Betta were leaving to go back to their flat, Granny whispered she wanted to speak to Anna alone as she had news for her. Once more, Giò offered to distract the two girls, who had returned to their games and were pretty distracted anyway, while a puzzled Anna followed Granny and Agnese into the kitchen.

"Dear child," Granny said to Anna, shutting the kitchen door behind them, "I spoke to Ornella, the president of a local volunteer association. They usually run a kiosk or two at the Christmas Market, and whatever profit they make is donated to a good cause."

"I'd be glad to help," Anna replied, with evident relief. She had learned to fear that any news could be bad news for her and her daughter. "I used to be rather good at making colourful balls to decorate the Christmas tree. I just wonder if I can find what I need."

"There's a shop in Sapri," Agnese informed her, "where you will find styrofoam balls. Are you going to be doing patchwork to cover them?"

"Exactly."

"Then I have scraps of fabric you could use, left over from shop window displays. But I think Gran wants to tell you something more about the Christmas Market."

"Well," Gran continued in an unusually soft voice, "the ladies have had their meeting and Ornella has agreed that this year, helping someone close to home would be the best use of the proceeds. We're thinking you and Betta should get all the money from the Pink Slippers Christmas stall, so once you get to Naples, you will have the means to spend some time adjusting to your new life."

Anna stood silent, unable to speak or move for a long moment.

"I'm so grateful, I really am," she finally mumbled. "But I don't think that's fair. I do have a job right now… I don't think it would be right to take more from you. It looks like charity, and maybe there's someone who's worse off than we are."

Gran took her hands. "Anna, frankly, what money do you have? A little something you saved these last few months?"

"Not really. In Calabria, we ended up spending the little I had to help Auntie Battistina…"

"Moving to a new city, getting settled and finding a job may turn out to be very expensive. Having a little nest egg to back you up once you get there will help you through."

Anna looked Granny straight in the eyes. "Still, it looks like charity, something I'm not sure I deserve." But Gran guessed there was a little hurt pride going on too.

"It's not always easy to accept help, I know. But you should also think of Betta."

"But I wouldn't know how to thank you, nor am I certain that I will ever be able to repay any of that money."

Granny laughed. "It's not money to borrow, it's a gift." And before the young mother could object to that, she added, "And you know, people who are lucky enough to receive help in life hardly ever repay those who bestowed the help on them. But…" she paused for a little while to allow her words to sink in and win over any resistance, "you may find yourself in the position to help someone else in the future, and that, believe me, is the best expression of gratitude."

Something in the second part of the speech struck Anna, who nodded silently. Granny kissed her on the forehead.

"Good girl. Now, let me see if I have a few scraps of fabric myself."

6 DECEMBER – WHODUNIT?

When Giò got up the next day, she saw the sun shining onto her terrace. In the distance, the sea was a deep blue, and she promised herself a kayak ride in the afternoon if she managed to put in some serious work on her travel guide all morning.

A kayak ride just before Christmas, go figure! What a cool place I live in. But that might be why I'm not feeling the Christmas spirit. I'm used to cold winter days, but maybe a green Christmas isn't all that bad.

When she arrived at the library, it was already open. Laura Libretto greeted her.

"Hello, Giò, how are you?"

"Trying to get used to the idea of a green Christmas."

"Last winter, the top of Mount Coccovello was white for a few days, but I'm afraid it was in late January. And six or seven years back, we had snow in the very centre of Maratea. It caused quite a bit of chaos, but it was beautiful. It looked like a place from a fairy tale."

"I remember Agnese sending me a few pictures of the snow on the beach. It didn't look real. But nice though it is to chat, I'd better get started," Giò added, sitting in her favourite place with her laptop and notes.

As the morning progressed, she edited, she wrote, she reread, for once satisfied with her work. At midday, she took a break and approached the shelves dedicated to Europe. Visiting the library earlier in the year, she had found a guide to Scotland written in the early 70s; she loved old guides because they gave her a feel for how much a place had changed, or not changed, and how people's perceptions had evolved. But today, the guide was not there.

She walked over to Laura, wondering who else in Maratea could be interested in such an old book.

"That's strange, I'm sure nobody borrowed it because I would have thought about you as soon as I saw it."

Laura searched the shelves and the returns trolley, then she and Giò had a look together through the travel and geographical sections, but the book wasn't there.

"Oh no, not again!" Laura cried helplessly.

"Again?"

"Yes, though it's usually children's or teenagers' books."

Giò looked at her without understanding.

"Yes, it's been happening for roughly a month now. Books keep disappearing."

"You mean someone is stealing books from the library?"

"Not really, since they reappear after a while. It looks more like they are borrowing them without coming over to the desk and filling in the forms."

"Why would they do that? Wouldn't it be better to borrow them properly without taking the risk of being caught and accused of being a thief?"

"It's been driving me mad. Initially, I thought I was imagining things. I believed books had disappeared, then a week later, they'd be on the shelves again in their proper place."

"Any new faces among the readers?"

"No, not really. It's always the same people and they all have a library card. I can't see why any of them would take the books in such a way."

"You said it's mostly children's books, so maybe it's a sort of dare – kids challenging each other to see if they can sneak books out unobserved."

"I can't imagine any of them doing that, but then again, I can't think of a better explanation."

"Do you run a complete inventory?"

"Only at the end of the year."

"So if there are other books missing, you have no idea?"

"No, it's only when someone asks me for a specific title that's neither on the shelves nor in the borrowing records. Then I know it's missing."

"How weird! I guess you'll have to keep a closer eye on the regular readers."

"That's what I've been doing, but with no luck so far."

7 DECEMBER – LIGHTS ON

"Already up?" asked Anna. She had gone into Betta's room expecting to find her fast asleep, only to discover her daughter was up and ready to go to school.

"Tonight they are switching on the Christmas lights. I can't wait! It will be so pretty. And Lilia told me the kiosks will be selling beautiful Christmas decorations, and they sell sweets and malt wine…"

"Mulled wine," her mother corrected her.

"Mulled wine, but it doesn't really matter since Lilia and I are more interested in hot chocolate. Lilia said they serve strawberry flavoured hot chocolate. Can you imagine anything as delicious as that? I can't, even if I do my best. I mean, I know what chocolate tastes like, and strawberries too. But strawberry chocolate goes beyond my imagination. Can you imagine it yourself, Mum?"

Anna stopped herself from saying anything, but a shadow must have crossed her face as Betta was quick to read her thoughts.

"I won't ask to buy anything, I'm already so happy to be here. But, Mum, I can look at all those pretty things… and looking will be enough. Even just knowing that something as good as strawberry hot chocolate exists makes me feel happy." She kissed her mum's face and sat down for her breakfast, chirping, "I can't wait for this evening to arrive as fast as possible. I wish school was already over."

Betta's happy mood was infectious and Anna found herself sharing her daughter's enthusiasm. By the time she arrived at Agnese's perfumery to start work that Friday morning, she was humming Christmas tunes under her breath.

∾

"WOW, THAT'S A LONG FACE!" TEASED GIÒ.

Paolo, the brigadiere of the local carabinieri, was sitting at one of the bar tables in an alley a short distance from Piazza Buraglia, the main square of Maratea where a team of workers were checking the last-minute details for the Christmas lights, the kiosks and all the decorations for the opening of the Christmas Market and the start of the festivities.

"Hello, Giò, will you join me for a beer?"

"No mulled wine for you?"

"Not today. I don't seem to be in the Christmas spirit."

"That makes two of us," Giò replied, taking a seat beside him. The bar was almost completely empty; it would be a different story in a couple of hours. "What's wrong?"

"You've heard about the recent thefts from villas locally? It's been going on for a whole month now. Thieves are raiding people's homes and getting away with it."

As a matter of fact, Giò had also heard people complaining about the carabinieri doing nothing about the spate of crimes, but she thought better of mentioning this to Paolo.

"Do you have any clues?"

"Nothing. It's an unusual method of... work."

"Yeah, from what I've heard, they aren't emptying the houses, just taking some jewellery."

"That's right. These are no common thieves – no PCs, no TVs. They seem to know what they want from each house, and exactly where to find it."

"Any likely suspects?"

"Not really. We checked with local police in the areas around Maratea, but we didn't find any similarities to these thefts."

"So the thieves have just started a new business here in Maratea?"

"They seem to be rather skilled, so maybe they come from further away than we think. But at the same time, they have specific information, almost as if they have insider knowledge..."

"I'm sure you'll find your way in this case. Just give yourself time."

WITH THE EXCEPTION OF DON ANASTASIO – THE LOCAL PRIEST who disapproved of the commercial side of Christmas and would only sneak over to the stalls for a glass of mulled wine when he naively thought nobody could see him – and the few unfortunate souls who didn't dare to contradict him, the whole population of Maratea was in Piazza Buraglia at 6pm to listen to the mayor's speech. But mostly, they were there to witness the moment the Christmas lights were switched on.

Maratea's mayor, Biagio Zucchini, wasn't the greatest orator in the world, but like most local politicians, he was absolutely convinced he was. He started by describing the great efforts the town officials had put into ensuring everyone could enjoy such pretty illuminations, thanking every single important citizen for their contribution – mainly other politicians in his party. He then felt he had to add a few words about the future of the town and his great plans to bring in more tourists, and not only in the summer – much like various mayors had been promising for the past 30 years. Following this, he became almost lyrical, talking about the values his family had instilled in him as a child, starting from his grandfather who had also been the town's mayor.

As the speech droned on, getting longer and longer, the children started to become impatient. And in fact, it wasn't only the children. At first, it was just a few whistles, then some shouts, but finally the whole crowd was chanting loudly.

"Lights on! Lights on! Lights on!"

Zucchini finally stopped, cued the technicians to proceed, and all of a sudden it was Christmas in Maratea. From the darkness, the huge Christmas tree, standing at the tip of the triangular piazza, glistened with its myriad white lights, spreading festive cheer all around. Then the lights in the streets were switched on, progressing down every single alley and bringing them all to life, each one with its own decorations. Finally it was the turn of the Christmas Market: the kiosks appeared in all their colourful glory, as if the hidden laboratory of Santa Claus had popped up, full of the beautiful creations the elves had been working on for the whole year.

As the crowd started to swirl around, taking pictures or wondering what to buy or eat, Luca turned to Lilia and Betta.

"Let's go to the Piazza Vitolo," he said.

"But I'd prefer to look at the market," Betta protested softly.

Luca shook his head. "We'll be back soon, I promise, but there's the angels."

"The angels?"

Luca and Lilia nodded with such enthusiasm that Betta was convinced. The market could wait.

When they reached the other square, a light and sound show was being projected onto the walls of the town hall. A dance of snowflakes and angels accompanied the Christmas tunes filling the air. Betta, having lived in Milan, was familiar with elaborate light shows, but the quaint little town, dressed up for the celebrations in its unsophisticated beauty, moved her far beyond anything she'd seen before.

And she wasn't the only one who was spellbound. Her mum, Anna, was watching the Christmas lights as she and Agnese were making their way back to the perfumery they had closed briefly to watch the ceremony. When Agnese asked her if she missed Milan and its splendours, Anna didn't reply, simply shaking her head.

When has greater meant happier or prettier? Hardly ever. Actually, I don't think I have felt this happy for a long time.

8 DECEMBER – CARTELLATE AND VINCOTTO

G ranny woke up earlier than usual; she wanted to get going in the kitchen to cook the Christmas cartellate for the Pink Slippers market kiosk. It was a long process, so she wanted to give herself a headstart.

To her surprise, when she entered the kitchen, Adelina was already there. Worse than that, she was standing in front of the wooden pasta board, mixing flour and olive oil.

Granny's eyebrows shot up to her hairline in dismay.

"Good morning, Adele, I thought you'd be getting some rest…"

"I did have a good sleep, thank you. But you know, it's better for the dough to rest a little before we start frying, so I set my alarm clock for 6am."

"Did you warm up the oil before pouring it into the dough?" Granny asked, wondering why she hadn't set her clock for 5am.

"Of course I did. Have your breakfast while I finish off here."

Granny checked the other pot on the cooker, slid the tip of

her finger into it and had a little taste. As she had suspected, it was white wine.

"I think we should turn this off or it will get too hot and the dough will lose elasticity."

"I've only just turned it on, it needs a good minute longer. It has to be warmed gently – if it's too *cold*, the dough won't turn out as light as it should." Adelina touched the liquid herself and shook her head, unconvinced. "There's some barley coffee ready for you, so why not have your breakfast and let me finish here?"

Granny sighed, picked up the Moka pot and poured the dark liquid into her cup, followed by a large drop of milk. She tried to look elsewhere, but her eyes kept staring at Adelina's hands working the dough as she slowly added more wine or flour.

"You should be more delicate or the dough won't turn out properly."

Adelina was sweating with the effort, but she knew what she was doing. And more importantly, to her at least, she was triumphant that the dough had been made according to her specifications, a variation on their mother's original recipe with 50 grams more flour, 10ml more oil and 10ml less wine. But any variation on a family recipe was a matter of endless quarrels between the two sisters.

"How's Giò doing after calling off her wedding?" Adele asked.

"Much better than when she was with that stupid fop…"

"Has she found someone here in Maratea?"

"Not yet, I'm afraid."

"You mean you haven't done anything yet? She's 38, she should get married. She needs a husband."

"I know, but these things take time. Women have become very difficult nowadays."

"I'm sure there are some widowers in Maratea."

"She had a crush on a divorced architect a couple of months ago..."

"Widowers are much better than divorced guys, they already know the rules. With divorcees, you never know..."

Granny nodded. "As a matter of fact, the guy ran back to his family. But I don't mind as I didn't think he was the right match for her anyway."

"You shouldn't waste any more time. You never know when she might decide to leave again."

"I know," Gran replied curtly.

"I'll keep an eye out at the Christmas Market and speak to the women there. There must be a nice widower in Maratea."

Gran added an extra spoon of sugar to her barley coffee. It was just a couple of days since her adored sister had arrived, and Adele was already meddling in her two most important realms: her kitchen and her matchmaking. She stirred the coffee vigorously; she didn't like interference.

"There it is," said Adele, looking at the shiny dough ball. "Not too soft, not too hard, just perfect. We could start with the first one I made while this second one takes a little rest."

Unconvinced, Granny gave the dough a pinch, but finally had to acknowledge it might do. She gulped her last drop of coffee and got ready to proceed, pulling out the drawer containing her rolling pin.

With mellifluous voice and mischievous eyes, she said, "I'm afraid I've only got one."

"Don't you worry, I brought mine," Adele said, revealing her own rolling pin that had been hidden under a cloth. And since they were even, Granny had to concede with some regret that they'd be better off using the pasta roller anyway. There was quite a lot of work to do.

"Not as good as a pin," Adele agreed, "but definitely much faster."

After a rather harsh disagreement on how thick the pasta

dough should be, followed by extensive negotiations, they decided to set the machine to three. Then they had to compromise on the strip lengths, as Granny liked larger roses while Adele preferred smaller ones. As the latter started to pinch the folded strip every three centimetres, Granny said that two and a half centimetres would be better. The pockets would be slightly smaller and stay crunchier when coated with grape must vincotto.

"Grape must vincotto? I've brought a couple of bottles of fig vincotto. It tastes so much better."

"Fig vincotto? No way."

"It's tastier."

"Fig vincotto was used during the war as a poor substitute for when grape must wasn't available."

"As was barley coffee, but you're still drinking it," Adele replied without hesitation. It was a hard blow for Granny to take.

"I don't like barley coffee. It's the doctor who says it's better for me than real coffee..."

"But you've always said you prefer it to real coffee..."

"That was only so Agnese and the kids wouldn't feel sorry for me."

The elderly sisters were still staring at each other fiercely when Agnese knocked on the door. Granny hid the pasta roller under a cloth as her granddaughter, on her way to the perfumery, kissed both of them with a cheerful smile. Then she looked at the wooden board in dismay.

"Have you only got ten cartellate ready? My goodness, I thought with there being the two of you, you'd be way ahead. If only you were using the pasta roller..."

Both older women took their rolling pins in their hands, as if they wouldn't entertain the idea of using a machine when they could do everything by hand.

"You know they need to dry for at least an hour before frying. I'd hurry up if I were you."

"That's exactly what I was telling your grandmother. If only she weren't so stubborn."

Agnese looked at Granny sternly. "Please, the two of you, don't start quarrelling. You have the whole Christmas holiday for that. Now it's time to help us with the Christmas Market. What will you be using for the topping?"

The answers came in unison.

"Fig vincotto."

"Must grape vincotto."

Agnese knew better than to get embroiled in their petty quarrel.

"Do some with the figs, others with the grape vincotto, and remember to have a third batch coated with honey. Some people don't like vincotto at all." She smiled at the two mulish cooks before adding sweetly, "And hurry up – please."

WHEN AGNESE CAME BACK AT 2PM, SHE WAS HAPPY TO FIND THE kitchen filled with trays of cartellate, nicely shaped into smaller and larger roses. Auntie Adelina and Granny were laughing and chatting amiably, and while one was frying the latest batch of cartellate until they were golden, the other was quickly immersing them in honey before placing them onto a tray.

But as Agnese tasted one from the must grape vincotto tray, she sensed the old tension coming back. She stuck her finger against her cheek.

"Delicious! Crispy and light, just as I love them."

Then she moved to the second tray and took a fig one.

"These are simply lovely. I wouldn't know which ones I prefer."

The tension vanishing again, the two elderly women smiled at each other and resumed their activities to finish the next tray.

As Agnese left, Granny said, "Agnese wanted to prepare the cartellate herself, but I told her no way. She's a good cook, mind you, but she can't make cartellate as good as Mother's. You see, she uses all the modern stuff. Nothing like the traditional way of making them."

Adele nodded. "She's never had the advantage of seeing our mother preparing them. Good cook as she might be, it's not the same as seeing them done first hand by an expert."

"And she uses the mixer for the dough."

Adele looked up to the sky. "My goodness, there's nothing to beat the warmth of your hands to make a serious dough."

"And she mixes oil and wine together."

"That's the young generation for you!"

At four o'clock, Nando went to Granny's to pick up the cartellate. Luca helped him to get the trays into the car and take them to the market.

"We prepared a few for you and Lilia so you can taste them tonight," Auntie Adelina said, giving him a smaller tray of honey-coated cartellate. Luca glanced at them.

"We'll be making more for Christmas, don't you worry," added Granny, reading his thoughts.

The boy finally smiled.

"They smell so good, the Pink Slippers will raise a ton of money with these."

And the cartellate were a real success at the market,

though some of the Pink Slippers members commented how different they were from their own.

"I don't mean they're no good," said Mrs Paloma Parasole, "but my family recipe adds some cloves in with the wine when you warm it up, and that gives off a delicious aroma."

"Our family secret," Mrs Ornella Capello, the indomitable president, had to have her say, "is to let the dough rest under a wet cloth for a whole hour before starting to cut the strips. It makes the cartellate slightly crispier."

Mrs Parasole, her shiny white front teeth biting into her fourth cartellata, replied, "I'm sure the roller was at three, which makes them slightly too thick for my taste. That's why I gently press mine with a rolling pin after they come out of the machine. They're just as crispy, but lighter, if you see what I mean."

As for the customers, they were dreamily biting into their cartellate and finding it hard to resist a second one as soon as they'd finished the first. Only once the last tray had disappeared did people notice all the arts and crafts on display in the second kiosk run by the Pink Slippers Society.

Mrs De Blasi arrived in front of the second kiosk, a big bag in her hands – far too big for someone so small. She handed it to Mrs Parasole.

"Besides buying a few things from you, I'd like to leave this for Betta. It's our family Christmas crib; I guess Betta will enjoy it much more than I do."

"That's so nice of you," said Mrs Capello, wishing she'd had such a good idea for a present herself.

"Betta will be delighted," Mrs Parasole added, storing the crib in a safe place inside the kiosk. But when she turned around, Mrs De Blasi had already disappeared in the loud, happy crowd.

9 DECEMBER – THE CRIB

"May I offer you a cup of coffee?" Anna asked, welcoming Giò and her niece and nephew in.

"A coffee with a generous drop of milk will be lovely, thank you."

"Then I'll get you some, and what about for you, Lilia and Luca?" But the siblings had already joined Betta and were busy contemplating the terracotta statues from Mrs De Blasi's crib.

"Where do we start?" Betta asked.

"Look what I've got here," Luca said, pointing to a large box full of stuff he'd carried from home. "I've brought some moss, some strings of electric lights, paper to make mountains to surround the crib…"

"And a starry sky," completed Lilia.

"Correct. So first, we should find a place to put the thing. Let me see how large the crib actually is."

With extreme pride, Betta took out the handmade cork Nativity scene and showed it to them.

"It's beautiful!" Lilia cried. "Granny would love it."

Luca, more pragmatic than his sister, took in the large

number of shepherds and other statues, then walked around the room, evaluating where would be the most suitable place for it.

"Well, I'd say this corner of the living room is perfect," he said, moving towards the chosen spot and looking over at Anna, who nodded in approval. "We need a couple of empty boxes to create the mountains. We'll thread the lights through them before covering them with the paper."

Using a large table as a base, Luca set out the three shoe boxes he had brought along to create the basis for the mountains. The girls looked disappointed, but the boy shook his head.

"This is the groundwork. You'll see – when we cover them with the moss and the paper, it will all make sense."

"Here's your coffee, Giò, and some biscuits made by Nennella with apples and cinnamon, although I think those two little girls are too taken with the crib to think about eating," Anna said, laughing.

"Well, I can eat and work at the same time," said Luca, busy passing the string of lights beneath the paper covering the 'mountains', and then inside a few model houses he'd perched on the heights.

"Look, this one is a mill, it should pass over a little brook," Betta said, pointing to the small construction, hardly believing all this could be hers.

"We need some tinfoil, and then you'll have your brook. I believe I also saw some fishermen somewhere."

Betta rushed to the kitchen to get the tinfoil, then looked on in amazement as Luca cut long sheets of it, folded it between his hands and created a little stream. It started off narrow over the mountains, only to get wider as it flowed down to the flatter part of the display. He then positioned some light bulbs so they'd reflect on the tinfoil as if it was water.

"You're not taking an active part in the process?" Anna asked Giò, who was sipping her coffee and looking at the children without interfering.

"They only brought me along to help clean up the mess, I suspect. I've no patience nor talent with craft work."

Anna looked at her watch. "I need to hurry, or Agnese will think I'm a lazy worker."

"Off you go," Giò said. "I'm afraid you might still find us here when you get back. There's a lot of work to do."

Betta hardly glanced up when her mother left. When Anna saw her so enraptured by the company and the atmosphere, a sudden fear flashed across her mind.

This is too much joy for us. Will it last? She shook her head and reproached herself. *Just be glad for now, live this dream.* And she made for the door, happy to be going to work.

BY THE EVENING, THE FRAGRANT EARTHY MOSS WAS IN PLACE. Luca had carefully hidden all the cables and the lights were peeping out in exactly the right places: all along the sparkling brook, with its ducks, fishermen and washerwomen; inside the little houses on the mountains; hidden between the moss and the lake he'd made with a piece of broken mirror. There was also a little light for each of the Wise Men, riding their camels towards the grotto.

"Luca, you're a master crib maker!" Giò clapped her hands, copied by the two girls.

"Now we can put the actual crib itself in its place," he said with pride.

"It's beautiful," said Giò, admiring it. "It's handmade, as things always were in the olden days."

The roof was made of cork, the walls designed to look like they had been cut from the rock behind them. On one side there was room for the Holy Family, the ox and the donkey, and beside the crib, two shepherds stood on a circular platform, maybe looking out for the Star of Bethlehem.

"This was automated," Luca explained. "The shepherds should go round, coming in and out of the stable, but I'm afraid it doesn't work any longer."

As he turned the wheel, a few notes came out.

"It's a carillon," Giò cried.

A carillon? How weird.

Luca held the Nativity scene in his hands and tried to move the wheel, but it seemed to be stuck and no more sounds came out of it. He slowly shook his head, looking up at the three pairs of expectant eyes in front of him.

"I don't think I can do much about it. Maybe we could ask Dad to have a look."

Giò approved with her usual enthusiasm. "Betta, would you like to have the carillon working properly?"

"Will you be taking it away?" Betta asked, disappointment showing on her face.

Giò looked at her watch. "It's 8.35. Your mum will be home soon. We'll show her the illuminated Nativity scene, and then if you want, we'll take the carillon to Nando and see if he can fix it. Does that sound any better?"

"Yes please, let me surprise Mum, and then you can take the crib away... for a day or two. It won't take longer than that, will it?"

"I'm sure Dad will fix it quickly. He is damn good. Tomorrow, you'll have it back." Luca knew how to handle the younger kids and Giò winked at him, choosing to ignore the D word. Agnese would not have approved.

The door knob turned and Betta cried, "She's coming!"

"Turn off the lights."

"Mum, don't come in yet. Wait for us to tell you it's OK."

When Anna was finally allowed in and told to open her

eyes, she gasped in surprise. The twinkling lights on the crib blinked on and off, each revealing a new detail: the little houses on the mountains; the baker pulling bread from a red-hot oven; the crib and the still empty manger. She had never had a crib in her house at Christmas before. This was gorgeous.

10 DECEMBER – A CARILLON AND A TUNE

When Agnese went to open her perfumery the next morning, she found a young woman standing in front of the door, waiting. Agnese had left home earlier than usual on purpose to have a few minutes by herself to do some of the accounting she hadn't done the day before, but it looked as if she might as well have had half an hour's more sleep.

She smiled nonetheless. "Good morning."

"Mrs Fiorillo, I'm so glad you're here early."

Agnese recognised the young woman, who worked as a housekeeper for some of the more well-off families in Maratea.

"Hello, Mariella, how are you doing?" she asked, searching for the shop keys in her bag and opening the turquoise shutters.

"I came over to see if you need any help in your shop for the Christmas season."

"I'm afraid I've already found my help for the season. Was it for a friend of yours?"

"Actually, it was for me," Mariella said sheepishly as they entered the shop.

"For you?"

"Yes."

"How come?" As far as Agnese knew, Mariella had always been rather proud of her housekeeping job.

There was a long pause before Mariella spoke, but at least the young woman helped Agnese push the rattan armchairs and a few Christmas decorations through the open door and set them out in front of the perfumery.

Once they were back inside, Mariella said in a faltering voice, "After I left the Rivellos, I soon found a new position with Mrs Lavecchia. We'd been getting along well, until a few weeks back... when she said that I had stolen her diamond earrings..."

"*What?*" Agnese couldn't believe her ears. Mariella was too smart – she had said so herself not two months earlier – to steal things from a house in which she worked. No one had ever complained about her before.

"The thing is that she found those earrings in the pocket of my coat but, Mrs Fiorillo, I swear, I've been doing this work for years, and I've never stolen a thing..."

"I know, I know. But how do you think those earrings ended up in your coat?"

"I haven't the slightest idea."

"Mrs Lavecchia has two nasty kids. I wouldn't be surprised if they'd played a cruel trick on you."

"I have to confess, that's what I thought."

"But with years' worth of good references, you'll have no trouble finding another family to work for."

"It's not that easy. I suspect Mrs Lavecchia has spread the rumour that I'm a thief, and no one I've applied to will take me. Then I remembered you were looking for some extra help for Christmas and you know me well enough..."

"I certainly do know and trust you, Mariella, but as I said, I've already found someone to help me. But I will speak to my customers and see if anyone is looking for a good and trustworthy housekeeper. Leave me your phone number."

"I'm due to get married next summer," the young woman sobbed, writing her details on Agnese's agenda, "but having the whole town thinking I'm a common thief is driving me mad. What will my mother-in-law think?"

"I'm sure she will trust you and her son more than Maratea's gossips. As for Mrs Lavecchia, with her kids, she should really be more careful about judging other people."

"She's been dreadful, she's ruined me and my family."

"I wonder why the other families you've applied to trusted her judgement more than your good reputation."

"It has come at such a bad moment. You know, with all these robberies going on in Maratea. People have become very suspicious."

"Calm yourself, dear, I'll make sure to mention all of this to my more trusted and influential customers. We'll sort it out, you'll see."

But as Mariella left, Agnese's face dropped. She was nowhere near as confident as her cheerful words had suggested. Mariella was right – the issue of the gang of thieves certainly exacerbated her bad luck.

GIÒ WAS REVISING THE FIRST DRAFT OF HER GUIDE TO SCOTLAND when the doorbell rang. Lilia and Luca stood on the threshold, smiling, and Luca held a box in his hands.

"Dad fixed it last night. The crib, I mean."

"I'd almost forgotten. So the carillon plays its tune?"

"It's so nice," Lilia giggled. "Shall we take it to Betta? I'm sure she can't wait to have it back."

"There's no point having the scene with no Nativity. Let's go." Giò put her papers in a pile and a pen on the last page she had reviewed, picked up her jacket and off they went.

"I was missing it so much," said Betta when they arrived, showing them the empty space in the crib scene. "Yesterday evening, after you'd left, we didn't switch on the lights. No point in doing that when the Nativity was missing. But tonight, Mum, no TV. We will just enjoy looking at the crib and telling stories."

Anna smiled.

"And you'll have music, too. Dad has fixed the carillon." Luca opened the box. Carefully extracting the crib, he put it back into its place, switched on all the small lights and turned the carillon anticlockwise.

Then he released it.

The two shepherds started to rotate. Inside the stable they went, then out again, their faces lifted up towards the sky while the first notes of the music drifted into the air.

They had been smiling, but on recognising the tune, both Giò and Anna became serious. How could this be? The carillon was playing exactly the same Scottish Christmas tune Betta had been singing a few days earlier – the tune her dad used to sing. Betta recognised the song as well, but it only added to her happiness as she started singing along.

"You'll have to teach me those words," Lilia said.

"So the tune isn't *that* unfamiliar in Italy," said Anna to Giò.

Giò shook her head. "If we asked around Maratea how many people knew it, I'm sure very few, if any, would say they did. This is just an incredible coincidence."

Her thoughts returned to the evening in the park and the robin on the tree branches. *Is there something important about the carillon and its tune? Am I missing something? Or am I going mad? Is it true, as Agnese and Granny say, that I cannot distinguish dreams from reality?*

"It's almost half past four, time for the shop to open," Anna said, looking at her watch. "I'd better go."

"Granny is waiting for the kids to join her and do their homework at home. Luca, can you accompany those two young ladies? I need a little fresh air, so I'll walk with Anna to the shop."

"Will do," said Luca seriously. He was very responsible whenever he was treated as a grownup.

When they had left the flat and the kids had gone on ahead, Giò said, "Anna, may I ask what made you come to Maratea? You were in Calabria and were heading towards Naples, so why did you decided to stop here, of all places?"

"That is a good question, Giò. Alex, my husband, rarely spoke of his past life. He used to say it was too full of painful memories. But once I found a postcard from Maratea in one of his books. It wasn't a written one, just a picture of the coastline."

"Was he from Maratea?"

"No, his family was from Rome, but when I asked him about the postcard, he said it was a place he'd stayed for a short while in his youth, and he'd loved it. He said that sooner or later, he would bring us here, but he ran out of time…

"I never forgot the name of the place, and when we decided to run away from Auntie Battistina, I realised we'd be passing not far from here. It reminded me of him. I just thought on impulse we would have his blessing on our new life if we stopped by. And that's exactly what has happened, for both me and Betta. Our time here has been the happiest we've had since Alex passed away."

"Did he say if he had any relatives or friends here? Why was he was so fond of this place?"

"I'm afraid he could be rather evasive. He hated speaking about his past, so I never met anybody in his family. All he told me was that he was an only child and his parents had died when he was young, and he had no other relatives. He was just as vague about Maratea."

"Didn't you find it strange that he wouldn't tell you about his past?"

"Oh, we had quite a few heated arguments, especially at the beginning of our relationship when I felt I'd never get to know him properly if his past was shut away from me. But then, he was such a perfect partner – a good husband and the sweetest father. I had no reason to doubt him. And I soon learned that if his past was so painful for him, I had to respect his silence."

"What was your husband's surname?"

"Giordano. Alessandro Giordano," Anna said. As they'd reached the perfumery shop, she added, "Are you coming in?"

"No, I need a walk. I've been editing all day, so I need to stretch my legs a little."

Giò had half a mind to think over her Scotland guide as she walked. She needed to alternate hours of intense concentration with time to distance herself from her project to see the direction it was taking and keep the thing moving. The reviewing process was more of a rewrite, which could be painful, so taking a walk was the ideal way to see if she needed steering onto another path or if she was doing fine.

But this afternoon, there was no room in her brain for work. The resemblance between Betta and Mrs De Blasi's son, the postcard from Maratea, and now the Christmas tune that Betta seemed so familiar with. Wasn't that worth investigating more than the umpteenth tourist guide on bonnie Scotland?

She walked a full circle around the park, only to stop at

the same bench she had sat on just over a week ago. And the robin was there again – he definitely kept late hours for a little birdie.

"Have you come to tell me something more?"

But the robin just jumped between the walls of ivy covering the otherwise leafless trees, a cool gust of wind reminding both that winter, even in temperate Maratea, had finally arrived.

11 DECEMBER – THE BOOK THIEF

When Giò had finished her turn manning the Pink Slippers kiosk at the Christmas Market, tourists were still flocking by. She decided to enjoy a little of the festive atmosphere as a visitor rather than a stallholder, and as she hadn't yet bought any Christmas presents for her family, maybe the market would help her with a few ideas so she could tick off some names from her list.

As usual, her eyes were drawn by the most exotic but useless things she could find. Where Agnese would have picked up elegant Christmas tree decorations, handmade terracotta statues for the crib, knitted woollen scarves or gloves, Giò spotted the odd – generally the ugly odd. Wouldn't Luca love that cuckoo clock with ghosts and witches instead of the usual Tyrolean figurines? Wouldn't Lilia be crazy for that shapeless red hat, topped with a snowflake pompom? How about a heavy copper cauldron for Granny? Its verdigris stains gave it such a traditional look.

Luckily, before she'd started her shopping, Giò met Laura Libretto, the librarian.

"Laura, how are you doing?"

"Fine! I'm enjoying the Christmas Market – it's the first chance I've had to visit and I've bought quite a few things. I've also tried the biscuits from the Trecchina bakery stall – they're so very good." Laura offered Giò one from a paper bag. Giò tasted it with an approving smile.

"Delicious! Agnese got a pandoro from them and it was scrumptious. In fact, I will have to buy another one. Maybe two as I don't think one will make it to Christmas."

One hour later, Laura was so overloaded with bags and presents and goodies that Giò offered to accompany her to her car.

"I parked in Piazzale Europa, it's more convenient for the library," Laura said, pointing towards a small pedestrian alley going downhill.

"How's your unconventional book thief?"

"He is still rather active, I'm afraid to say. I suspect he operates when the library is closed, but there are no signs of a break in. On the other hand, I'm sure none of the people who come in regularly have taken anything away with them surreptitiously. They all have their library cards and I've been watching them more closely than ever."

"This is so strange. Shall we go and have a look now? Just to make sure there's nobody there."

Reaching Laura's car, they left all the bags and parcels in the boot and walked the short distance to the library, entering through the gate that gave onto the garden. From outside, everything looked normal. The main door was closed, the windows too. They peered in through one of the windows; everything was as dark and quiet as they'd expected.

They were leaving when Laura gave a soft gasp. "There!" Giò looked back at the nearest window and saw the light of a torch moving across the volumes on the library shelves. Then the torchlight stopped moving, as if the thief had laid it on the shelf to keep his hands free so he could browse through the pages of a few books.

"It must be a child. The torch can't be any higher than the third shelf," Laura whispered.

"How did he get in?"

"I've no idea. The door and windows are locked. Unless... unless he used the toilet window. But it's so very small, only a cat could get in from there."

"Let's go and have a look!"

In silence, Laura showed the way. Giò switched on her phone light to have a quick look, making sure it wouldn't be visible from the library reading room. The toilet window was rather high up, but the thief had placed the garden ladder against the wall in order to break in.

"He will come out the same way he went in. I suggest we wait here."

A few minutes later, a rucksack was launched from the small window. Then a little shadow squeezed through the tight space, moving fast with the agility of a weasel. When he touched ground, the small boy recovered his rucksack, put it on his shoulders, and then took the ladder to put it back where it had come from.

It was then that Giò pointed her phone light into his face and moved towards him. But before she could say a single word, the boy dropped the ladder and ran away, climbing the garden wall as quickly as a wild animal.

"It's OK, we don't want to hurt you, come back!" Giò cried, opening the gate and looking out onto the street, but her request was vain. The boy had disappeared into the darkness.

"I shouldn't have scared him with the torch."

"I believe I recognised his face," said Laura, joining her. "I'm sure he is a Roma boy I've seen in town with some older boys."

"Do you think he belongs to the camp that moved here in mid-November?"

"That's about the time when the books started to go missing."

"Some people suspect the Roma are responsible for the recent thefts from local houses."

"Some people shouldn't be so quick to judge! The housebreaking is a matter for the police to solve; I'm a librarian, so I'm only interested in my readers. We have a boy who's keen on reading, we scared him, and I can't allow that. I can't lose any readers, especially nowadays."

"Maybe he's not a reader; maybe he's selling the books."

"No, Giò, the books are always returned in good condition. He is a respectful reader, and he can read quite fast, too. We need to find him and tell him he can come to the library whenever he wants."

"I'm not sure some people in Maratea would appreciate what you're saying."

"I never bothered about the opinions of narrow-minded people when I was young, so I'm not going to start now I'm in my sixties. Would you accompany me to the Roma camp, Giò?"

"Of course I will. Not too sure what we will achieve, though."

"Could you meet me tomorrow at one o'clock in the library?"

"I'll be there," Giò replied.

They checked the library room. As Laura had expected, everything was in order. On the children's shelves, she found the missing copy of *Matilda*.

"You see, Giò, he's returned the book, and it's in perfect condition," Laura said triumphantly. Giò nodded and indicated it was time to leave. Accompanying the librarian back to her car, she confirmed their arrangements for the next day, but turned down Laura's offer of a lift back to the upper part of the village.

"I think I'll walk," Giò replied, wanting to think over the scene she had just witnessed and what to expect the next day. She feared the Roma people would be rather hostile, especially when she and Laura said they suspected one of their children had broken into a protected place.

If Paolo were to hear of our plans, he would be mad at me, but I'm not going to get involved in his investigation into the jewellery thefts. That's for the carabinieri to solve, but I won't leave Laura to visit the Roma by herself.

Giò shrugged. Fate was always putting her in uncomfortable positions.

12 DECEMBER – THE ROMA CAMP

"What are we going to tell them?" Giò asked Laura as they parked close to the Roma camp.

"Since I've no idea how they are going to take to us being here, I have no plans. Let's see what happens."

As they got closer to the caravans and tents, a couple of dogs started barking. A few people came out to watch them pass, others looked at them from behind their windows. The two women could see curtains twitching on either side of them.

Finally, a tall, robust man came forward – dark eyes, dark skin, proudly contemptuous.

"Good morning," Laura said cheerfully.

"Morning," he replied sulkily. "What do you want? Are you from the social services?"

"Social services? No, no, we're from the library in Maratea."

"Library?"

"Yes, the library. I believe one of your children was interested in joining us. We have a meeting for children on

Saturday afternoons and wondered if you'd allow him to come."

The man laughed. "You mean... things to do with books?"

"Yes, we read out loud from children's books. It's called the Story Hour and I believe..."

"Well sorry to interrupt, but our kids are not interested in books. That's a thing for gadgies..."

"Gadgies?" Giò repeated.

"That's what we call the likes of you, who do not belong to our people," he snorted scornfully. "You see how we live." He pointed to the camp around him. "Here we're lucky to have water, but you wouldn't exactly call it luxury. We need to fill our bellies first, so we've no time for books, believe me."

"I've no doubt an empty stomach takes priority, but I'm sure you still enjoy music and dance. Stories are not that different."

The man looked at her. "We can play violins and guitars, but most of us can't read more than a few words. Books aren't meant for us."

An older woman came forward. She had a round tanned face with smooth skin, but there were dark circles around her eyes.

"Who's there?" she asked the man.

"Social services, asking about the kids and books," the man replied curtly.

The old woman's eyes flamed. "You're not going to take away our kids."

"As I was saying, we're not social services at all. We're from the local library and we came over to invite your kids to join our reading group on Saturdays."

"They don't know what they're talking about..."

"Shut up, Gabriel. How did you come up with such an idea?"

Laura and Giò looked at each other, uncertain how to answer.

"I think at least one of your children loves books," Laura said. "I want him to feel free to come to the library whenever he wants."

"It's cold. Come over to my caravan, I've got a hot cup of tea ready."

"Watch out, Maria, don't trust those town women," Gabriel said as Laura and Giò followed the old woman.

Despite the mud and puddles all around the camp, the caravan was sparklingly clean inside. Following Maria's lead, the two visitors removed their shoes as they climbed in. An uplifting perfume of herbs and tea filled the air.

Once they were sitting at the table, without the eyes of the Roma on them, Laura told the old woman the story of the child who came at night to borrow books from the library.

"Do you mean he's stealing things from the library?" the woman asked, still unsure whether to trust them or not.

"Not a single thing," Laura reassured her. "He always returns the books he borrowed in perfect condition."

"I think I know who he is. Wait a second." Maria left her caravan, coming back a few minutes later holding a small, skinny boy by the hand. Giò immediately recognised the scared little face she had seen in the torchlight. Undoubtedly, the child recognised them too. His eyes dropped to the floor as if searching for his toes, and beyond.

"This is Jonas," Maria said. "My grandson."

"Hello, Jonas, we're glad we've found you." Laura smiled at him and told him about the Saturday meetings, but the boy didn't answer.

"I don't think he likes the idea of meeting the other kids. We Roma are never well received, I'm sure they will tease him."

"All I can say is that your grandson is very welcome in

Maratea Library." Laura smiled at Jonas again. "If you don't want to come when there's too many people around, I'd advise you to come in the morning when the other kids are at school."

Jonas still didn't reply, keeping his eyes on the floor.

"It's nice of you, but your people won't like him being there."

"I'm the one who decides who can and can't come into the library. If anybody says or even hints at something nasty to Jonas, I will ask them to leave immediately. This is my promise."

For the first time, Jonas looked Laura in the eyes.

She continued, "You can continue to borrow any book you want. We appreciate that you have always returned them punctually. But last time, you forgot your library card."

She put a new library card on the table and wrote his first name on it. Bewildered, Jonas glanced at the card, and then at the old woman. When she signalled to him to take it, he picked it up, enthralled. He looked as if he had received the greatest gift ever.

"You can go now," the old woman told him.

The child whispered, "Thanks," to Laura and Giò in such a low voice, they couldn't be sure he'd actually said anything. But there was a sparkle in his eyes that said much more than words.

"He doesn't go to school, does he?" Laura asked.

Maria shook her head. "Like most of our kids. We're nomads, changing places all the time. And anyway, most people wouldn't be happy if our children were in the same classes as their children."

Laura didn't preach. She accepted the words of the Roma woman and drank her tea.

"It's delicious."

"And it will keep away any cold. My grandmother taught me how to recognise good herbs."

"How did you know," Giò asked, "it was Jonas who came to the library?"

"Jonas lives with his father and dreams of becoming a doctor. He lost his mother, my daughter," she added, barely concealing a sigh, "to appendicitis – we asked for help from the hospital, but only when it was too late. It's difficult for us to approach your kind, even in emergencies."

"How did he learn to read?"

"I have no idea. Some of our kids do attend school every now and then, so maybe he was one. Jonas is very clever."

"I've no doubt about that," Laura said. "And is Jonas a typical Roma name?"

For the first time, a tiny smile appeared on the old woman's face. "No, it's a Jewish name. Jonas's great-grandfather and a Jewish man helped each other out during the Second World War. They both got away from SS soldiers and made it to England, promising to name at least one boy in each generation with each other's first name. We've kept to our word."

"Such a heart-warming story," Giò cried.

"I'd be happy if Jonas kept visiting my library," Laura said, finishing her tea. "As I said, in the mornings there aren't many people there."

"It's up to him. We will not prevent him from coming if he's happy there."

13 DECEMBER – STAINED GLASS

Giò had been at home all day. If she wanted her manuscript to be finished before Christmas so she could be free for the two weeks of holidays, she really had to work hard. Her editor wanted it back on 7 January.

Editing had always been tough for her, harder than writing. By nature, she loved to start new projects, but she was not 'a finisher'; she'd had to learn those skills, because if she wanted to create something good, she had to care for it from beginning to end.

"Perfection is in the details," she'd repeat to herself in her lowest moments, but it took some effort for her enthusiastic nature to maintain the discipline to concentrate on the little things when her mind longed to be free to create something new.

But today, the fact that she had something she wanted to do as soon as she finished her work had been a tremendous help. She wanted to visit Maratea's cemetery before it closed at sunset, and the thought had kept her motivated. By half past three, she had finished her 30 pages of edits and was ready to go.

Maratea Cemetery looked like a small village to Giò, maybe because the chapels resembled old houses, the cypresses making up the gardens. She had always liked to walk through cemeteries; they were full of stories to tell, but today she had no time to meander among the tombstones, nor browse the loculi – the typically Italian walls with their niches fronting head-on coffins to save space in the burial grounds – reading names, looking at pictures and dates of birth and death. No, today she was on a mission.

She approached the cemetery keeper and asked him where she could find the De Blasi family mausoleum. The man accompanied her to one of the side alleys and pointed to a group of private chapels on the left.

"You will find it open. It's a request of the family that visitors can walk in. I will close it 15 minutes before the cemetery shuts down for the night."

Giò found a white mausoleum with a certain air of grandeur. After all, the De Blasis were an old Maratea family, and one of the richest too. She pushed the elegant wrought-iron gate and went in.

As she got used to the darkness inside, the first thing she spotted was an elegant marble altar at the bottom of the inner chapel. Behind it, a long, narrow window with decorative stained glass featured a dark green forest and a robin sitting on one of the lower branches of a tree.

"You again," Giò said, smiling at the bird.

The last of the afternoon sun was hitting the glass, sending colourful reflections around the altar cross and onto the stone paving at her feet. On her right there were some votive candles and freshly cut flowers. It was a pity the chapel was too dark to have plants growing.

I'd rather have a simple grave under the grass with a little plant beside me than such a dark, imposing mausoleum.

Above the flowers were the loculi niches, covered by

commemorative wall plaques in white marble. The first one belonged to Ermanno De Blasi, the husband of Mrs De Blasi who had died just a few years back. He had a rather severe face, but then again, the portraits on tombstones always tended to be solemn. It was not acceptable to smile, let alone laugh in an Italian cemetery. Above Ermanno De Blasi was his son, Marco, who had died in 2005, well before his father. An only child, he had passed away when he was twenty years old. What a tragedy for his parents. All their riches had not been enough to ensure a little happiness for the family.

Oh my goodness, Mrs De Blasi was right. As Giò looked at the picture of Marco, she realised the resemblance between him and Betta was striking, especially as the picture had been taken when the boy had been about the same age as Anna's daughter. Betta's familiar features, her bone structure and concentrated expression, stared back at Giò from the wall plaque.

But he died when he was 20, so why use an image of him when he was a boy? Tradition dictated you use a recent picture of the departed, not one taken over ten years earlier, especially when the departed had been so young.

Giò looked at the empty space, possibly waiting for Mrs De Blasi to join the rest of her family. *I'm not sure I'd like to see that if I were her. On the other hand, life hasn't been easy for her so perhaps she's ready.*

On the opposite walls, there were more plaques. Giò ran her eyes over those, scanning names and dates, trying to guess who they were. The last one was for Elisabeth McAndrew, born in Scotland. A Scottish ancestor – a Scotswoman had lived here in Maratea. Imagine that?

Giò smiled. She had always liked the idea of people from different cultures mixing. Had Elisabeth come over as a young girl or a grown woman?

Then Giò stopped. *Scottish? Did that explain the tune in the crib, the song that Betta knew from her father?* This was a discovery.

A sudden knock on the door made her jump.

"I'm sorry, Miss," the cemetery keeper said. "I didn't mean to scare you, but it's time for me to close the chapel."

Giò returned to the Christmas Market where she had volunteered to help out on the Pink Slippers stall for the evening. It was the night of Santa Lucia, the shortest night of the year according to tradition rather than accurate astronomical facts. People were in church at the moment, but soon they would swamp the streets and the market with their chatter and laughter. The atmosphere was getting more Christmassy each day, but still Giò wasn't really feeling it.

She had gone to the cemetery hoping to find a connection between Marco De Blasi and Alex Giordano, but one had died in 2005, ten years before the other. Could Mrs De Blasi have had another child? Maybe the black sheep of the family, disowned and unmentioned? This was an interesting lead she would have to follow up.

14 DECEMBER – A CRUEL FATHER

For the second day in a row, Jonas was sitting at one of the desks in the library, reading. His lips were moving silently, as if pronouncing the words would help him to immerse himself in the world he was reading about. Laura watched him, considering the speed at which the boy was turning the pages of the book. He was a fast reader for a seven-year-old, especially as he had received little formal education.

Jonas wouldn't speak to her, not out of indifference, but because he was a very shy boy and his relationships with the non-Romani world hadn't always been easy for him. In the library, he had chosen a desk close to the bookshelves and far from all the other desks, despite the fact that they were mostly empty in the mornings.

Today, Laura, when she wasn't spying on Jonas, was busy reading the Compulsory Education Laws about the possibility of home schooling, wondering if the little boy could be involved in such a programme. The people in his community wouldn't be able to help him with his studies, but maybe local libraries could find volunteers to help him wherever his family took him.

At midday, Jonas left, borrowing two books. As usual, he didn't speak, but smiled sheepishly in response to whatever Laura said to him. On the threshold, he met Giò coming in.

"Soon I won't need to read any more, I will just ask Jonas for all the answers," she said. The boy looked up at her proudly, showing her his two books, and then ran away almost as fast as he had when they'd first discovered him in the library. But this time, a happy grin was stamped on his face.

"He's a cute little scamp," said Giò.

Laura replied seriously, "I'd love him to attend school wherever he is, but that's not always possible…"

"The authorities don't allow it?" asked Giò, moving closer to the library desk.

"Most schools would be open to Roma children, but often there's nobody to take them in on time for the lessons, and the camps are too far for the kids to walk to school. Also, I believe Jonas didn't like the one school he went to. He is an extremely sensitive child."

"So what's on your mind?"

"Schooling for children is compulsory in Italy, but it can take the form of home schooling."

"But Jonas's community won't be able to instruct him."

"He only has to take an exam at the end of the year. The authorities aren't bothered who prepares him."

"I'm not sure," said Giò, dropping her bag close to the desk. "No matter how clever Jonas is, he can't prepare for those exams by himself. He's just a child and he needs some guidance, if only to understand what the exams will be about. There's such a gap between formal education and knowledge as such…"

"Of course. I thought of that and I was wondering if the

libraries could help. They might give private lessons to Jonas every now and then."

"It will be chaotic. Each library will have its own approach, the child will be totally confused."

"I'm hoping that once he's done his first exams, Jonas's confidence might increase enough to convince him to go to school. But for now, he could try learning this way. If the worst comes to the worst, he will still have learned a few things."

"What will they say in his community?"

"Knowing Maria," said Laura, thinking of the old woman's attitude, "I think they will leave the choice to Jonas."

"What about the other kids?"

"Most of them don't attend schools, and if they do, it's not regularly. Often they're merely tolerated, not properly assisted. But I believe some of the other kids could learn from Jonas. They may even decide to go with him to the libraries to be taught by the volunteers." Laura opened a drawer in her desk and pulled out a workbook. "I left a maths book for him between the pages of a book he was reading. He found it and did some of the exercises. There were a few mistakes, but he learns fast. I say it would be a pity not to help him as much as we can."

"HELLO, GIÒ, PLEASE COME IN," SAID MRS DE BLASI.

Giò looked around the large living room, its formidable library of books made up of colourless volumes. Heavy curtains framed the windows, and on the walls were a number of portraits and ancient landscapes in oils, housed in richly ornate gilded frames. Maybe it was the overall grandeur or the dark antique furniture, but there was something intimidating about the room.

"Can I offer you a cup of coffee? Something else to drink?"

"A cup of tea, please."

"Lemon and sugar?"

"Both, please."

As Mrs De Blasi left, Giò's eyes wandered around the room again. What struck her was the lack of photographs. On a canted console table, she finally spotted a single picture. It was the same photo she had seen in the mausoleum, portraying the young son.

When Mrs De Blasi came back, Giò was still contemplating the photo.

"My goodness, no wonder you thought about your son when you saw Betta. The resemblance is striking indeed."

"It was such a surprise, so unexpected. I confess I only saw my son…" Mrs De Blasi blushed slightly, putting the silver tray on a low table between a mustard yellow sofa, where she invited Giò to sit, and the armchair where she sat herself.

"How old was he in the picture?"

"Ten years old, not much older than Betta."

"I saw this picture yesterday in the graveyard," said Giò, feeling slightly embarrassed. She didn't know how to approach the conversation; she wasn't even sure what she was investigating or where she was heading.

"Yes, it's the same picture." Mrs De Blasi's simple answer didn't help.

"Do you have other pictures? What did he look like when he was older?"

"Unfortunately, I don't have any other pictures." Mrs De Blasi sighed heavily, drank a sip of her tea, then slowly put the cup down on the table. "My husband destroyed every memory of my boy. I was lucky that the mum of one of his friends had kept this single picture."

"Was this after your son had died? Was your husband trying to assuage his grief?"

"Not at all," Mrs De Blasi said, somewhat sharply. "You see, Giò, my husband was not an easy man to live with. He was a domineering, possessive man, a real tyrant, and I was meek and stupid, a sort of puppet in his hands. My son rebelled and left home as soon as he came of age, and he never came back."

"Oh, and how did he die so young?"

"He died in a fire in Milan. He was…" She sighed again, a tear rolling down her cheek. "He was a vagrant. His father had to go and identify his body. But to answer your question, it was when Marco ran away that my husband destroyed all his belongings, all his books, baby clothes, every single photograph."

"How old was he when he ran away?"

"He had been running away for years, but when he was younger, his father would use his parental authority to get him back. Once he was 18, Marco disappeared without trace, but a year later, my husband managed to find him. My son was already in Milan, working and studying at the same time, and they had a major fight. My son told my husband his days of slavery were over and that he'd better disappear from his life. When he came back, my husband was raging as I'd never seen before, and God knows how many times I'd seen him mad. It was then that he destroyed everything Marco had left behind. Every single memory."

"And you never got in touch with Marco?"

"We did write on occasions, but after the quarrel, my husband made me write a letter to Marco, an awful letter where I disowned him as my child."

"I'm so sorry I've brought up such sad memories."

"It's good to speak of it; it puts things into perspective when I talk them over with someone. When I'm all alone, I just blame myself for having been so weak. In his last letter, Marco was mad at me. He told me to consider him dead, that he wished he had been an orphan right from the start. And we never heard from him again."

"How did your husband take it when Marco died? Did he ever repent?"

"The man didn't know the meaning of the word. He didn't even want his son buried in the family chapel. He insisted he had no son, that he only went to Milan to identify the body to do his duty as a responsible citizen, not as a father. I moved Marco's body into the chapel after my husband's death. In truth, I wouldn't have moved him there at all if it hadn't been for his Grandma Elisabeth. He simply adored her. And she was the only one who could mitigate my husband's violent spells. But it was not only because of that – the protection she gave Marco, I mean. The two of them shared a beautiful relationship. She taught him to play the violin and they enjoyed telling each other stories. My mother-in-law passed away too early – I wish I had died instead of her. She would have been a better mother to my son, and I have no doubts he'd still be alive."

"Don't say that! Blaming yourself won't solve anything. I know it's very hard to deal with bullies such as your husband. But tell me, is it because of Elisabeth that the carillon in the crib plays a Scottish Christmas tune?"

"Yes. My father-in-law was very much in love with his wife, and when she moved here to Maratea to marry him, he asked some local artisan to design a beautiful crib, expressly requesting that the carillon played that tune. Here, as in Naples, we have very talented crib makers. The gift was a way to combine the Scottish and the Italian traditions."

"It was generous of you to donate that to Betta."

"I won't lie to you, I'm particularly drawn to that little girl. It's not just because of her resemblance to my son, but... it's hard to explain. There's something so familiar about the way she says things, the way she moves." Mrs De Blasi smiled. "Maybe I'm just getting old. I've had such a lonely life, it's easy to get sentimental. In any case, I'm going to keep in touch with them. Anna is a proud woman and I don't think she will allow me to do too much for them, but at least they know they can count on me for help at any time."

"That's sweet of you, I'm sure it'll be good for the two of them. They were very lonely before they arrived in Maratea, but they've found a few good friends now. But what about you? Don't you have nephews and nieces?"

"Like my husband and my son, I was an only child, so no. I was left without a relative in the world when my husband and son passed away."

Giò played her last card. "So you didn't have any children besides Marco?"

"Luckily not," Mrs De Blasi answered, shaking her head in denial.

"Sorry if I persist, but did you never fall pregnant again? A miscarriage perhaps?" Giò felt her cheeks blush as she asked the question.

But the way to the truth is never a comfortable one, she encouraged herself.

"No, never," Mrs De Blasi answered, looking almost shocked at Giò's suggestions. "I was at least spared that."

"I apologise for having been so blunt," Giò said as she left, all her hopes dashed. It seemed there was no link whatsoever between Anna's daughter and Mrs De Blasi's family.

15 DECEMBER – WHO WAS HE?

"Paolo, how can this be?" Giò asked as they sat comfortably at one of the tables outside Leo's café. "I have searched for Alex or Alessandro Giordano, Anna's husband, but I haven't found much. Actually, I've found hardly anything."

"Strange," replied the other, slowly sipping his espresso. "Nowadays, thanks to the internet, it's almost impossible not to leave tracks."

"Well, to tell you the truth," Giò's cappuccino and cornetto had been sitting untouched in front of her for an unusually long while, "I only found a few things relating to the last years of his life, but nothing from earlier. Where did he come from? Where did he study? Did he have any relatives?"

"If you give me his full name, place and date of birth, I could do some research for you," Paolo said.

"I do have all those details. In fact, I was hoping you'd offer to do just that." Giò sent him the details via a WhatsApp message. She herself had extracted the information from

Anna and her daughter separately, nonchalantly asking them seemingly insignificant questions about Alex.

"Let me have a look in our system and I'll get back to you. But why are you so curious about him?"

"I have half an idea buzzing around my brain. If it proves to be a dead end, I want to be able to close the door on it once and for all. I need final confirmation, that's all."

"Hmmm, I see, you don't want to tell me more. You're sleuthing by yourself." He glanced at his empty cup, then at Giò's cooling cappuccino.

"I'm sure there's nothing behind it, so there's no reason to waste your precious time," she babbled before switching the conversation onto another subject. "How about your investigations into the thefts?"

"We're getting nowhere," sighed Paolo, his shoulders drooping as his slightly chubby figure squirmed on the chair. "We can't find any trace of the stolen jewels, even using informal channels and asking the regional carabinieri to help us track them. As for the thieves, they know how and where to strike with minimum effort for the greatest loot."

"A new Arsène Lupin?" Giò smiled.

"It's no joke. People in Maratea are scared, they feel their homes aren't safe, and how can I blame them? There's nothing worse than feeling insecure in your own home…"

"Having your house broken into is certainly not a pleasant experience. I'd feel very vulnerable – if I owned anything worth stealing, I mean."

"Yes, and when people are scared, they're prone to do stupid things, believe anything to apportion the blame."

"You mean blaming an innocent person?"

"Exactly."

"Yes, Agnese told me that Mariella, the housekeeper who used to work for the Rivellos… do you remember her?"

Paolo nodded, remembering a previous investigation that

had seen him and Giò working together for the first time. "Of course I do. What about her?"

"Apparently, Mrs Lavecchia accused her of stealing her precious diamond earrings…"

"Wasn't Mariella the one who bragged that she'd never be so stupid as to steal things from the houses of the people she worked for?"

"That's right. But since Mrs Lavecchia accused her and fired her, no one has wanted to hire Mariella."

"I see, another innocent getting all the blame," said Paolo angrily.

"What do you mean by *another*? Who else has been suspected?"

"There's a mounting rumour that all these thefts started when the Roma arrived in Maratea. Quite a few villagers are convinced they are responsible for breaking into the houses."

"Oh my goodness!" Giò immediately thought about Jonas and his camp. "But is there any proof?"

"None so far. The thefts are out of the ordinary. Common thieves would normally take anything that could be converted into money, not necessarily the most precious things. And then there's the method the thieves have used to enter and search the houses, as if they knew all the how-tos in advance. No, I don't believe it's the Roma, but they will get the blame if we don't find the real culprits very soon."

16 DECEMBER – A NEW LIFE

"I'm afraid we could find nothing." Paolo was sitting at his desk in the carabinieri station. He'd felt the news he had to tell would be better communicated in a safe place, without the risk of eavesdroppers.

"What was that?" asked Giò, turning her head at every noise.

"Don't you worry, Giò." Paolo smiled. "Maresciallo Mangiaboschi will be away for the whole day…"

Giò smiled back sheepishly at her fears being so obvious.

"To answer your question," Paolo went on, "we can't trace his family. We know he was born in Rome, had a common first name and surname, but his documents, ID card, National Health System Code, Tax Code – they all pop out of thin air 11 years ago."

"Is that unusual?"

"It is. Normally, people apply to renew their ID one year, their driving licence another, their NHS card another. I only know of one reason why all the evidence of a person's life would start in the same short interval of time, when there's nothing before. Can you guess what that reason is?" He paused meaningfully.

"Come on, spit it out!" said Giò, irritated. "I don't have time for your riddles."

"I thought you'd already got there," Paolo couldn't resist provoking her further, "and only needed my confirmation."

"I haven't a clue. And now you've got me to admit how ignorant I am, Mr I-know-it-all, would you please illuminate the darkness around me with the light of your knowledge?"

Paolo knew better than to feel intimidated by her sarcasm. "Only if you promise to tell me everything about how you came to your conclusions."

"You really don't deserve it, but this time I've got no choice. I'll have to give in to your demand."

Paolo flashed a satisfied smile and said, "It's a case of a new identity."

"Please, explain further."

"Pretty straightforward, in theory at least. If you want to disappear and not be found, you can ask the government to give you a new identity. If they accept your request, you're given a new name (possibly a very common one), a new place of birth (possibly a densely populated city), and starting from there, you can apply for all your essential documents at the same time."

"Can anybody ask for a new identity?"

"Nope, it's not such a straightforward process after all, unless you can prove your life is being threatened or your birth name could cause you untold trouble."

"I'm clear about the first example, not so much about the second one."

"Imagine you're the child of a notorious serial killer whose name keeps on cropping up in the national media…"

"OK, got it!" Giò said. "Can you find out his real identity?"

"That's not going to be easy at all," Paolo replied, shaking his head. "If the government grants someone a new identity, they have to make sure the new identity can't easily be connected to the old. All you can do is start a special procedure and reveal your reason for the investigation, and then someone in government will have to judge if it's a good enough reason to uncover the mystery."

"Well, our man has been dead for two years, so nothing we discover can harm him now."

Paolo shook his head again, unconvinced. "But his family is still alive, and there's a minor too. What if she could be damaged by the revelation? What if some Mafia or Camorra member took revenge on them? Believe me, it's not an easy lead to follow. But it may make things easier if his wife were to make the request."

Giò looked at him, startled. After a little pause to think about it, she said, "I'm not sure I want to ask Anna to do that, nor would I want to expose her and Betta to any kind of danger."

"Wise girl." Paolo's phone rang and he pressed a button to summon one of his subordinates. "Please, Strazio, answer incoming calls for me. Make sure to take down the callers' names and messages, and I'll ring them back in 10 minutes." Then he looked at Giò's thoughtful face. "But you still haven't told me why you're investigating Anna's husband. Did she ask you to?"

"She didn't, it's all my own initiative." Giò waved her hand, a gesture she typically used when she wanted to avoid a particular subject.

"Can't you elaborate further?"

Giò sighed, realising it was too late to renege on her promise to reveal all. "It's… it's just some strange things have been happening," and she told Paolo about Mrs De Blasi being so shocked by the resemblance between Betta and

Marco, and how she herself had been to the cemetery and discovered Marco's portrait.

"But when did Marco pass away?"

"Thirteen years ago."

"And how old is the child?"

"She is eight years old and her dad only died two years ago."

"Then what are you investigating? I don't understand."

"Frankly, I don't know. That's why I didn't want to tell you. But I feel there's something that's eluding me, and…" she paused for a while, making sure she had his attention, "there are too many coincidences. Anna stopped here because her husband, whose real identity we know nothing about, had kept a postcard of Maratea. He was born in Rome, he lived in Milan, but he promised to take his wife and daughter to Maratea some day."

"Well, it's a lovely stretch of coastline here."

"Then we have the child who bears such a striking resemblance to Marco. Her name is Elisabetta, like the grandma Marco was so very fond of."

"Wasn't his grandma called Elisabeth? Wasn't she English?"

"Scottish, not English," she corrected him sharply. It still drove her mad when people referred to the whole of the British Isles as England and every one of the rich variety of people who lived there as English.

"Scottish, English, whatever! But one: her first name was Elisabeth, not Elisabetta; two: Elisabetta is a rather common name… it's not like Berenice or Artemisia."

"I haven't finished yet. I heard Betta singing a traditional Scottish Christmas song, which may be familiar in the UK, but I don't think there are many kids in Italy who'd know it word for word. Her mum tells me Betta's father, Alex, taught her. He always used to sing it at Christmastime."

"Come on, with the internet nowadays? Or maybe her father was passionate about Scottish folk music, and by chance, Mrs De Blasi's mother-in-law was from Scotland. I can't even call this 'evidence' thin."

"Wait! Good investigators keep an open mind. What would you say if I were to tell you that Mrs De Blasi gave her son's crib to Betta…?"

"That she's a very generous woman. Look, Giò, I need to get back to work." Paolo stood up, gesturing towards the massive piles of paperwork sitting on his desk, waiting for him. "I've always said you have a keen cop's hunch, but this time I fear you're on a wild goose chase."

"You interrupted me before I could finish." She held his gaze with rebellion sparkling in her green-yellow eyes, irritated that he wouldn't listen to her. "What if in that crib there was a carillon? And guess what?"

"It plays the same tune the kid was singing? It can't be."

"Bingo! You got there, finally."

Paolo sat down heavily. "That's weird." He let out a prolonged sound, the same expression of amazement he'd used as a kid when he heard incredible news. "Life is strange at times."

17 DECEMBER – A RUDE AWEKENING

It was early morning when the carabinieri surrounded the Roma camp, positioning their cars to block any attempt at a getaway. While some stayed to guard the perimeter, others knocked on the caravans' doors. There were shouts; there was panic; there were a few Roma who rebelled against the authorities; there were those who tried to run away, only to be blocked; there were babies crying.

Two hours later, the carabinieri had found nothing – no evidence whatsoever that linked the Roma to the stolen jewels. It was fortunate that the carabinieri hadn't resorted to violence, but when they departed, they left a hostile feeling behind. Some carabinieri were still suspicious, stating loudly that the Roma were too smart to keep the stolen goods with them. In turn, the Roma felt that no matter what they did, they would always be outlaws in the eyes of the authorities.

Laura Libretto was in the library when she heard the news of the early morning raid on the Roma camp. She waited to see if Jonas would show up, but there was no sign of him that day. When she got ready to close the library at lunchtime, her eyes fell onto the little desk far from all the others – the one Jonas had selected as his own. It looked sad and empty.

Maybe it's only for today. After all, the search has just taken place. I'll see what happens tomorrow. But in her heart of hearts, she feared she wouldn't see the bright little Roma boy in the library again.

18 DECEMBER – THE MAN WHO CAME FROM AFAR

G iò checked her mobile and read the text: "*Can you meet me at Leo's in 15 minutes?*"

"*Any news?*"

"*Some news, see you there.*" Paolo would say no more.

Giò was still in her pyjamas; she just had time to take a quick shower and get dressed before rushing out. From the door of her flat, it took her five minutes to get to the central square, which was already pretty busy. People were flocking in to go shopping; Christmas was getting very close now.

Paolo waved at her across the crowded square. He was already seated at a table.

"You could have chosen a quieter place," grumbled Giò, joining the chubby carabiniere. "I guess you've nothing confidential to discuss."

"On the contrary, but this morning the station is buzzing with curious carabinieri, so I thought there would be no better place to hide than in plain sight, blending in with the crowds of people whose minds are distracted by long lists of Christmas presents, their menus, their guests."

"You're the expert, I guess," said Giò, a rather sceptical

expression painted across her face. She hardly had enough room to pull her chair out and take a seat.

"What are you having?" he asked.

"Shall we go for an aperitivo? It's almost lunch time."

"That will do me. What are you drinking?"

"A glass of red. And you?"

"Just a soda. I'm working later, I'm afraid."

"I'm working too." Giò laughed as the waitress went off to fetch their drinks. "But in my case, the wine helps the creative flow." She raised the glass the waitress had just placed in front of her. "Salute!"

He looked sadly at his Crodino, but his face lit up when the food arrived. Leo's aperitivos were renowned for being not only mouth-watering, but also so bountiful, they could easily make up a proper lunch. As ham and mortadella cubes, bruschetta, panzerotti, olives, and sautéed chicory appeared on the table, Paolo gleefully tried one mouthful then the next one.

"I managed to get some info, Giò," he said eventually. "But I'm afraid this time, I was right – you've been chasing a wild goose."

"How come?"

"Well, apparently the man who took Alex Giordano's identity came from a little village close to Pordenone. He had lived as a vagrant most of his life, then in 2007, he asked for a new ID, and Alex was born."

"You said this was confidential information the government would be unlikely to disclose."

"Well, as it happens, I have a friend in the government office, and since he knows what a trustworthy cop I am..." His grin stretched from one ear to the other, but at Giò's stern look, he moved on. "In this case, the new identity was granted to erase a past of alcohol and drugs, a few petty robberies and a homeless life. The guy had managed to turn his life around, so the judge afforded him the possibility of a new identity."

"What was the guy's name before he took up the new identity?"

"Davide Bortolin, born in Pordenone in 1982, light brown hair, green eyes, height 1.76m. A past record of a few robberies, jail, but since 2005, he'd been clean. He'd found a job in web design, was somehow reborn. Two years later, he asked for and was granted the new ID. He kept on the straight and narrow from then onwards, becoming a successful graphic designer. His story could have had such a happy ending; a pity he should die so young."

"But his original family?"

"He was orphaned at a young age and brought up in a childcare institution, too much of a rebel for either adoption or a foster family. At a young age, he was labelled as disturbed – our Alex never had it easy. Nobody would ever have bet on him doing something with his life. You're not going to say anything to Anna, are you?"

"I thought we'd track her husband's origins back to Maratea, but as things stand, there's no point in me telling her anything we've discovered. If her husband never revealed anything about his past – and now I understand why – I certainly don't have the right to do so."

"But you're not eating at all." Paolo pointed to her untouched food. She had not even touched the panzerotti.

"It's the disappointing news, it's ruined my appetite. Now I feel as if I was wrong to have asked you to do the searches. I'm uncomfortable at knowing more about Alex than his wife and child do; I should never have poked my nose in. I had a feeling right from the start this wasn't going to be an easy Christmas."

19 DECEMBER – AN IMPORTANT YEAR

Giò woke in the middle of the night. There was something bothering her about the story of the poor devil who had managed to turn his life around and become the fine man Anna would meet a few years later. All of a sudden this man, Davide, labelled disturbed from childhood, had found the strength to leave behind his past of drugs, alcohol and crime and get a steady job... not easy for someone living on the streets. What had happened to cause this change?

Giò turned over in bed a few times, then realised she wouldn't be getting any more sleep that night. She switched on the light and picked up the note Paolo had given her, reading the man's description again. Alessandro Giordano: height 1.76m, light brown hair, green eyes, born in Rome, no distinguishing features (what a pity). Then she moved on to his bio, stopping on the date when he'd landed his first job in a small firm specialising in web design: September 2005.

What a shame that the man who'd had such a tough life but had managed to save himself and go on to have a family who loved him should die so young. It was very unfair, a missed happy ending. As the bright lightbulb above her and her thoughts set her logical mind to work, the feeling of discovery, of having found a thread that could solve the puzzle that had forced her out of bed, disappeared.

Light is the destroyer of dreams, she thought, going back to bed and switching off the bulb. But her brain refused to go to sleep. She kept thinking of Betta, the child with the enchanting green eyes, so similar to Marco's. But she wasn't related to him. Giò recalled Mrs De Blasi's shock when she'd first seen the child. It wasn't an illusion, born out of a mother's desire to see her son again; since Giò had seen the photograph of Marco, she'd known without doubt that the striking resemblance was very real. Betta's bone structure, her expression and, as Mrs De Blasi had said, the eyes. The same green eyes.

In 2005, Davide Bortolin had landed a good job. From the streets, he'd walked straight into a high-tech career. No matter how simple his position was, he'd had no formal training... wasn't this most heart-warming story a bit too incredible? And why did 2005 ring a bell?

Got it! Wasn't that the year Marco had passed away in Milan? Yes, she was sure it was. And in the same year in the same city, a young homeless man would change his life for the better. Marco's story kept intruding into other people's, bringing him close to Anna and Betta before taking another turn. Or was it her imagination playing tricks on her?

It was 4am. She couldn't call Paolo in the middle of the night, could she? Of course she could.

He replied after numerous rings.

"I thought a carabiniere would jump to action, ready to respond to an emergency."

"Who's there?"

"Dude, it's me, Giò."

"What the heck? What time is it?"

"I just realised that Marco De Blasi died in Milan at the exact same time that Davide Bortolin landed his job in web design."

It was a little while before Paolo replied. "So what?"

"I'm not sure, I just find it weird…"

"Maybe it's because it's the middle of the night and my brain is refusing to do anything but sleep, but I can't see any significance in that. In Milan, people emerge from the depths and others sink all the time. It's the big city rules."

"You're right, but…"

"What?"

"I wonder, can you find a picture of Davide Bortolin?"

"From his past records? Of course I can. You don't want to show it to Anna, do you?"

"As the only photos you'll be able to give me are likely to have been taken in prison, that would be too cruel."

"You're always stirring things up. Are you sure about this?"

"Of course I'm not, which is why, with the exception of you and Agnese, nobody knows anything about my research. But one step at a time. How long will it take to get the photo to me?"

"Strazio is on duty tonight," Paolo said, yawning loudly. "He'll help me out. I can have something for you by 7am."

"Something? The picture, you mean?"

"Without it, you'd never let me in."

"You're right." Giò chuckled as she ended the call and picked up a book. She knew she would get no more sleep tonight.

AT 6.30AM, PAOLO RANG HER DOORBELL. HE WAS EARLY, THANK goodness; she could wait no longer. He had a bag full of

warm cornetti from Leo's bar with him; he knew how fond Giò was of those. But despite the delicious fragrance permeating the air, she simply asked for the photo.

"You will find the whole thing strange," said Paolo, extracting three pictures from an envelope and putting them on the table. "These ones are a profile and front shot of Davide Bortolin when he was arrested at age 21, and this was when he was 17 and staying in a correction centre for minors."

"Oh my goodness!" Giò said, looking at the photos and sitting down in shock. "It makes no sense."

"Well if, as you say, Betta looks just like her father, and you hoped to find a striking resemblance between Bortolin and Betta, then no, it doesn't make sense."

Giò picked up her mobile and showed Paolo Marco's photo, the one on his tomb. Paolo nodded.

"In this picture, I can see the resemblance. This boy and Betta are like two peas in a pod. But he was about the same age as Betta in the photo, and sometimes youngsters with similar colouring can look like they're related. As for Davide Bortolin, maybe as a little boy, he looked more like his daughter…"

"To change is one thing, but there's no resemblance at all between Betta and Davide Bortolin," Giò said, looking again at the pictures on the table. "Nose, chin, bone structure – all different. Would the use of drugs have altered his features so much?"

"It could have done."

"But no," said Giò, shaking her head, unconvinced. "Anna always said how alike father and daughter were. Why would she say that if the two were so different?"

"Could it be that Anna emphasised a similarity that wasn't there, simply to keep the memory of her husband alive?" suggested Paolo. "It would be only natural, after all."

They fell silent, Giò looking up at Paolo. He was clearly just as puzzled as she was. Something wasn't adding up in the way they had expected.

"A betrayal? Anna had Betta by another man?"

"Sounds unlike her," Giò replied without hesitation. "Unless she had Betta before she met Alex – or rather, Davide – and he agreed to adopt her."

"But why would she speak so freely of the resemblance between Alex and Betta?"

"An attempt to cancel out the past?" Giò said without much conviction. "How I wish I could show Anna these pictures."

"I guessed that." He extracted a fourth picture from the envelope.

"What a weird portrait!"

"Well, there's been a bit of Photoshopping done in a hurry. It's the prison portrait, given a more civilised setting."

"I see. It doesn't look like a picture taken by the police, so I can show this one to Anna and see how she reacts without destroying the image she has of her husband."

"Exactly!"

"And if she recognises him, I will say that the picture was taken here in Maratea and invent some story. Then she'll be happy to be walking in his footsteps." She looked at her watch and sighed. "It's still only seven o'clock. It will be a good two hours before she's in the shop."

"Don't I deserve breakfast?" complained Paolo, pointing at the bag of now cold cornetti.

"Definitely," said Giò, absently switching on the oven to warm them, and then preparing the Moka pot for a strong coffee.

～

"SEE WHAT I FOUND," GIÒ SAID, EMPTYING HER BAG AND showing Anna the old picture postcards she had bought from the Christmas Market. "This is Maratea as it was 30 years ago."

"Not too different from now, I'd say," said Anna, looking at one of the postcards and reading the stamped date.

"We've been lucky," Giò agreed. "No development plans."

"And what are these?"

"I guess they're just photos of tourists who've visited here. Sort of selfies of the time. The local photographer kept copies."

"I love the way they used to dress, such a care for detail. And these are more recent ones."

"They were all mixed up on one of the stalls."

Anna returned the pictures to Giò. "I think Betta would be delighted to see them. But I'd better carry on with my work. I need to put all the jewellery away – a customer wanted to try all our earrings and necklaces. Do you mind?"

"I'll help you," Giò replied, smiling on the surface, but inside she was puzzled. Anna had looked at the picture of Davide Bortolin who – according to Paolo – had become Alex Giordano, her husband, but had showed no sign of recognition. Where had she and the carabiniere gone wrong in their investigation?

"I keep thinking how pretty your daughter's eyes are…"

"Same sparkling green as her father's," replied Anna without hesitation. "They were not only the best friends ever, but looked so much like one other."

"You'll have to show me his picture."

"I don't have many, he didn't like to be photographed. And he was a good photographer, so he was usually the one taking pictures of the two of us. But if you help me here, I do have a couple of pictures of him on my mobile."

"I promise I won't interrupt again till we've sorted all the trinkets."

Anna took out her mobile and showed Giò a portrait of a handsome man in his late twenties. He was hugging Betta and their two smiling faces looked up at the photographer, showing their striking resemblance. Giò enlarged the photo on the screen to have a better look at his face, gulping in surprise. There was no way the man in the picture could be Davide Bortolin.

Seeing the surprise on Anna's face at her reaction, Giò spoke quickly. "Dad and daughter really do resemble each other. Now I know what you meant."

Anna smiled. "And now back to work."

Giò followed her mechanically towards the counter, but her mind was in tumult. Alex Giordano was not Davide Bortolin. They were two different people, no doubt about that. But then, why had the government system linked the lives of the two people? It had complicated her investigation instead of helping her. Or maybe Davide Bortolin was a red herring to further protect Alex Giordano's real identity. What had happened in Alex's life to merit such extreme measures? And had she any right to try to uncover the mystery, or was this latest complication a warning she'd better leave things as they were?

"DESPITE DAVIDE BORTOLIN HAVING THE SAME GENERIC FEATURES as Alex in his ID photos, such as height, light-brown hair and green eyes, I can't imagine two men looking more different," hissed Giò, standing in a little alley not far from her sister's perfumery. "And Anna looked at Bortolin's photograph without a flicker of recognition. Alex and he had nothing to do with each other."

"This is strange," replied Paolo. He had been summoned by Giò with some urgency. The wind was getting up and he shivered as he held on to the small parcel she had requested. "I checked his profile again. The man in our picture – Davide Bortolin – asked to be given a new identity, and this new identity is registered in our system as Alex Giordano."

"Could there be a case of mistaken identity? Maybe there was another Alex Giordano who started a new life."

"I don't think so. The link on the papers was to our Alex Giordano. I'll do some more research, but it doesn't sound hopeful. Do you have a better hypothesis?"

"Could it be that the government wanted to further protect Alex Giordano's previous identity so they threw in a decoy?"

"That's more my line of thinking. You see, even the protective system can have some 'holes', and in special cases you want to protect people more thoroughly."

"You mean from nosey carabinieri asking their friends who a certain guy really is?"

Paolo laughed. "Exactly. In this case, we're simply friends trying to do their best to help someone. But imagine if we wanted to hurt Alex's family. Maybe Alex Giordano's former identity was in grave danger."

"Can you imagine if we were to find out he was involved with the secret services and doing something to help the country?"

"A sort of hero?"

"Well, it'd be a nice Christmas present for Anna and Betta."

"Maybe they're not meant to know any of this, for their own good."

"He might have had a dark secret, you mean?"

"We don't know. And you might think of me as a coward, but there are times you should stop looking, Giò."

"OK, I will stop trying to extract any information from the government. But I'm still free to prove a silly idea right or wrong. It's buzzing round my mind, and has been ever since we started this new identity investigation. If I'm proved wrong, I will accept the government had reason to protect Alex's past, and I swear I won't do any more sleuthing."

"And what's this new theory?" he asked, holding out the parcel in his hands. Giò ignored his question.

"If I should be right, I'd love to have proof ready to give as a Christmas gift, and I knew only the carabinieri would have a kit to hand…"

"I've really no idea where you're heading this time," said Paolo, not letting go of the parcel as Giò reached out to take it.

"There are a few things on my mind, starting with the carillon."

"The carillon?"

"Yes, listen." And Giò moved close to him and explained all her theories and bold ideas. Paolo shook his head in disbelief.

"I would say that's wishful thinking rather than a theory." Then he gasped. "You haven't one single shred of proof so don't raise people's hopes." Finally, he conceded defeat. "And you swear, with your hands in full view, no fingers crossed behind your back, that if this theory doesn't hold true, you will let things go and do no more sleuthing?"

"I swear, if we get negative results, I'll drop the whole affair and let things follow their course."

"THIS IS GIÒ BRANDO. MAY I COME UP FOR A SHORT WHILE?" said Giò into the intercom.

"Hello, Giò, you certainly may."

As Giò went in, Mrs De Blasi didn't show any surprise to

see her, despite the fact this visit followed closely on the heels of Giò's previous one. But the way she said, "How are you?" suggested she realised there had to be a significant reason for the younger woman to be there.

"I'm doing fine. Actually, I've just started an essay about small communities in Southern Italy and their roots in the rest of Europe. I'm looking for volunteers to take a non-invasive test that will show the origins of our local families, and I wondered if I might ask you. The test takes less than one minute and simply requires a little of your saliva."

"I'm not too sure I've understood the purpose of your research, but I'd be pleased to help."

"I have the kit with me," Giò said, extracting it from the parcel Paolo had given her. "I'd love to send my samples to the company before Christmas."

"Just tell me what I need to do."

Using a similar cover story, Giò convinced Anna and Betta to take the same test. As the two left the perfumery for lunch, Giò threw away Anna's test and, with the help of Agnese, hurriedly prepared a parcel for a courier to pick up.

"A speedy service at Christmastime, good luck with that," Agnese said as she signed the courier papers.

"Let's hope for the best. Paolo has asked for the express service – unofficially, of course. The company will know it's urgent."

20 DECEMBER – FAMILY SQUABBLES

G iò knocked at the door of Agnese's flat the next morning. The kids were already on their way to school, and she had been enlisted to work in the perfumery till Christmas.

"Am I taking you away from your work?" Agnese asked, letting her sister in before finishing clearing up in the kitchen.

Giò, unusually amenable, reassured her sister. "Nope, I've had enough of writing and editing and racking my brains. I need a change and to *do* things rather than thinking."

Agnese was satisfied. There was generally nothing she feared more than having her sister in a Miss Contrary mood in the shop, but there was something else worrying Agnese today. As soon as she had finished in the kitchen, she sat beside Giò and gave her the bad news.

"Just one thing before we go," she muttered. "Valerio called me early this morning. He said they won't make it for Christmas."

"Again?" shrieked Giò.

Agnese nodded.

"But he promised Granny that they'd come this year."

"I haven't told her yet. She was so happy that this Christmas would be like the old times with you, Valerio and Auntie Adelina here – the whole family."

"I guess it's Emmegra again, wanting to spend Christmas with her family and not allowing Valerio and the kids to be with us. She's such a selfish, stuck-up woman."

Agnese nodded lightly. "I mean, I know her side of the family wants her there, but once every few years, it'd be nice to let us have a get together."

"Her family, fiddlesticks! They live in the same place as them all year round. Nothing's going to happen if the four of them come to us for Christmas."

Agnese smiled, but thought better of reminding her sister how many times she had not spent Christmas with them because of a certain Dorian Gravy. Giò's former fiancé had not liked either Maratea or her family.

"Shall I tell Granny and Auntie Adelina?" Agnese asked finally.

"The sooner, the better," Giò sighed. "The two loves are planning to cook God knows how much to appeal to everyone's tastes."

"And to show off which of them is the better cook. Competition in that kitchen gets fierce this time of year."

Giò was too heartbroken to smile. They left Agnese's flat and knocked on Granny's door on the ground floor. Without preamble, they broke the news to the two elderly women.

Auntie Adelina was furious. "That Emmegra, I'm sure it's her. Again!"

"Valerio has no say in that family. The only one making decisions is that spoiled, heartless brat of a woman," Granny added. "And she promised that this year, they would make it to Maratea for Christmas. I haven't seen Giorgia and Giacomo in ages."

Agnese tried to contain the fire. "I'm sure they will come for New Year's Eve."

"New Year is not the same as Christmas," grumbled Granny.

"Not at all," Auntie Adelina agreed. "And we've spent so much time putting together a menu for Emmegra, considering all the allergies she suffers. It's a tough job to cook anything for her that's not grilled chicken breast and salad."

"I know. I'm mad myself, but let's look at the positive side of things. This year we have Giò with us, and you, Auntie Adelina, and we have Anna and Betta. It will be like the Christmases of old with plenty of people around."

But Granny and Adelina both shook their heads, unconvinced. "When we were young," said Granny scornfully, "there had to be over 30 heads sitting around the table for it to be a real Christmas."

"The good old days are gone," Auntie Adelina added.

"So we mean nothing to you?"

"Don't be silly, Agnese," said Auntie Adelina. "Of course we appreciate you keeping up the traditions…"

"Certainly," added Granny, "if Giò was married and had her own kids, it would have made things more bearable."

Giò was stung. "Agnese, we'd better move on or I might start saying things I will regret later."

"Was it necessary to say that in front of Giò?" Adelina asked Granny as the two younger women left for the perfumery.

"It was just to get rid of them. We need to act fast."

"But what can we do?"

"Didn't you mention you saw Emmegra liking a bag on Facebook a couple of days ago?"

"Yes, an ugly and outrageously expensive Tucci bag."

"I'm sure it's stocked in her favourite shop in Rome. Let's check it out."

The two women opened Granny's laptop, making sure they knew exactly which bag Emmegra Brando had liked.

"If she's put on her timeline that she likes it, it must be for a reason…"

"She's bought it, or she's going to buy it very soon," Auntie Adelina concluded. "And now what?"

"First, I'll phone the credit card company to make sure she bought it."

"They will ask for the card details…"

Granny winked at Adelina knowingly. "I took a picture of them a while ago. I knew it'd come in handy," she said, lifting the phone and dialling a number.

"Italian Express Card, what can I do for you?"

"Hello, it's Emmegra Brando here. I'd like to make sure that I haven't been charged twice for the same transaction by mistake. I've received two different SMS alerts. Is it possible to check it out?"

"Of course, may I have your card details?"

Granny read them out.

"And could you give me the Security Code? It's a three digit number on the back of your card."

Granny moved to the second picture on her mobile and read that out.

"And can you confirm that you're Emmegra Brando, born on the…"

Granny gave Emmegra's date of birth.

"And now the security question: what's your favourite fashion item?"

"Tucci bags."

"That's correct, Mrs Brando. So you wanted me to check your latest transactions?"

"One of the latest ones in The Snob Boutique, Via Corrotti, Rome."

"That's for 1,248.65 Euros?"

"Correct. The shop was very busy and I fear I might have been charged twice…"

"No, Mrs Brando, I only see a single transaction."

"OK then, I was just puzzled as I received two different SMS alerts about the same purchase."

"Maybe the phone lines were busy and they sent you the same message twice, but you were only charged once."

"Thanks a lot, dear, you've been very helpful."

"It was a real pleasure, madam. I wish you a merry Christmas and happy New Year with many more transactions using your favourite credit card."

"Same to you, dear, merry transactions," Granny replied, putting the phone down and turning to her sister. "Ouch, these people no longer know the real meaning of Christmas."

"But we were right?" asked Adelina.

"Of course, 1,248.65 Euros."

"If only Valerio knew," Adelina murmured conspiratorially.

"Oh, that would be unfortunate," added Granny, clasping her hands together. "He'd be so mad at her, what with the mortgage on the new house – the huge one she insisted they buy…"

"She promised she'd give up making crazy purchases, at least for the first five years, if only he agreed to the big house…"

"In the posh neighbourhood of her dreams."

"And he kept his promise."

"But she didn't, it seems. Would it be too bad of us to tell Valerio?"

"Absolutely! It's Christmastime and we should behave as nicely as possible, even to people like Emmegra."

"You're right, my dear," said Granny, amiably patting her sister's shoulder. "In fact, I'm going to phone Emmegra and congratulate on her splendid new Tucci bag."

21 DECEMBER – GOOD NEWS

"I can't believe it!" Giò roared, cutting off her phone call and slamming her mobile onto the table at Leo's bar, where she was having lunch with Paolo. She, Agnese and Anna had been working hard all morning in the perfumery and were taking it in turns to have a lunch break.

"What's the matter?" Paolo asked.

"The lab has run the test, but for privacy reasons, they won't tell me the results by phone, nor by email. We just have to hope the courier comes on time. The parcel is already on its way, and it should be here by the 24th if the courier does his job properly. I wish there weren't a weekend in between now and then."

"It may be that the test will say the two samples are not compatible. It would have been more definitive if we'd had the father's DNA."

"Thanks for cheering me up," Giò grumbled. "Let's hope for a bit of luck."

❧

IN THE SHOP, AGNESE AND ANNA WERE BEING ASSAULTED BY customer questions while busying themselves gift-wrapping, spraying perfumes, and advising on the best creams or trendiest make-up. Mrs Monaco, a middle-aged woman who seemed to have the weight of this troublesome world on her shoulders, despite everyone knowing she had an easy and privileged life, was begging Agnese to wrap her presents faster.

"You see, there's no one at home, and I'm just so afraid…"

Agnese looked up at her quizzically.

"Haven't you heard the news about Mrs De Fino?"

"No, what news?"

"Yesterday night, she and some other women went to play Tombola and Mercante in Fiera at Mrs Lavecchia's, and both Mrs De Fino and Mrs Agosto's houses were ransacked. They lost their jewels, their precious silver cutlery, chandeliers, tea service and all."

"How awful!" Agnese said, tearing too hard at the ribbon she was using for the present. "Oh so sorry, I'll do it again and I'll be quick."

"It looked like the thieves knew exactly where everything was. In under two hours, they'd raided two houses. Now you see why I'm in a hurry."

"And the carabinieri just sit and watch," added a young woman who was waiting for her turn to be served, her old-fashioned dress clashing with her modern high heels.

"We're the only ones who can protect ourselves from these strange people around town."

"I know it's maybe not the best of times, but I was wondering if you were still looking for some help at home…?"

"Oh no, I've got my old housekeeper back," Mrs Monaco cut Agnese off. "She's asked for an outrageously high pay rise, she's lazy and a walking disaster, but at least I know she's honest."

"Honesty has no price," the second woman replied, nodding vigorously, "especially these days."

No matter how many attempts Agnese made to help Mariella, and she had tried a number of times in the past few days, none had yielded results. Poor Mariella. If only the carabinieri would catch the real thieves, it would bring an end to this mass hysteria.

Agnese was still busy serving both customers, wrapping up Mrs Monaco's last gift, when the phone rang.

"Valerio, is that you?" she said as she answered it. "Would you mind if I called you back later? We're very busy just now," Agnese added as Mrs Monaco snorted loudly, sending her a furious look. But Agnese carried on speaking into the phone for a bit longer.

"OK, if it's very short... You're coming? For Christmas? Really? That's wonderful, Gran and Auntie Adelina will be delighted. Let me go now, but thanks for the splendid news!"

While placing each present in its own bag, accepting the payment and answering a flurry of questions from three different customers, Agnese managed to pass the news on to Giò, who had just come back from her lunch break.

"Finally, our brother has learned," said Giò with a grin, "how to make his opinion heard. He is a Brando, after all."

22 DECEMBER – NOT HEROES

It was late in the evening when Mrs Laura Libretto closed the library. Despite the huge Christmas tree adorned with brightly coloured pencils and copybooks the children had decorated, despite the cheerful displays on the desk and every single windowsill, she left with a heavy sigh. It was almost a week since Jonas had last visited; he hadn't even resorted to his old system of borrowing the books unofficially. Since the day the carabinieri had searched the Roma camp, he had disappeared. And she had been so busy with the library's Christmas activities, time had run away from her. Otherwise she would have gone to speak to the Roma before now.

Laura had just got into her car when she saw two young men coming towards the library, peering over the gate and walking around the garden. They had an air about them she didn't like in the least. Out of the car she climbed, and approached them.

"Hi, is there something wrong with the library?" she asked sharply.

"Not now, but we want to be sure," the larger of the two

said, stepping forward and puffing out his chest. "You can relax, no thief will dare come back here."

"I beg your pardon? Are you police officers in plain clothes?"

"No, there's simply not enough police to prevent crime in this town. We're just citizens volunteering as vigilantes."

While Laura was perfectly happy with volunteers helping the local authorities, especially when public funds were cut short, there was something about these two playing at being coppers she didn't trust.

"There have been lots of thefts from local houses recently," the man added. Tall and lanky, he had his fists on his hips and stood with his legs wide apart. "The carabinieri have no idea where to start, so we're taking care of things. We're protecting people like you." He obviously expected the older woman to compliment him on how safe she'd feel from now on.

"I'm not sure I want to be protected," Laura replied sternly.

"You should, if you know what's good for you," the shorter of the two said, standing beside his mate and assuming the same bold stance.

"Oh really? Please, could you explain to me why that is?"

"Well, you know, it's the gypsies. Since they arrived, they've been raiding the houses of decent people."

"We don't know it's them. In fact, when the carabinieri searched their camp, they found no evidence whatsoever."

"Those guys are smart." The lanky one's arms left his hips to accompany his words with all sorts of hand gesticulations. He seemed to think they were necessary to make this woman understand. "They don't keep hot stuff with them; they've already sold the loot or hidden it in a safer place. We want them to leave Maratea, the sooner, the better."

"If there's no proof they've done anything wrong, they have as much right to stay here as you and me."

"I can't believe you're defending them!" the shorter man said. "If only you'd seen what that sly little chap we caught was up to."

"Which chap?"

"One of the young thieves. He wanted to come into the library when our kids were in there. God knows what he had in mind."

"You mean a little child was coming in here to read some books, and you scared him off? What have you done to him?"

"We just told him to go back to his caravan and stay away from the town." The lanky one felt it was better not to add that he had taken the child by the collar and given him a good shake, growling into his scared little face.

"How dare you! I know who this child is – he's got a library card, as have all regular visitors to my library. You had no right whatsoever to send him away. You should be ashamed of yourselves, playing the strong men with a little one. But you're not going to get away with it. I'm going straight to the carabinieri to report what you've just told me."

"Hey, madam, don't get mad. It was for your own good. We didn't know gypsies could have a library card."

"It's such an act of cowardice to bully a defenceless child. And two against one. Do you know no shame?"

The word 'cowardice' finally hit home with the two bullies. They had regarded Jonas as a thief, a dangerous enemy, and they had felt like heroes for tackling him. Now this woman was pointing out that he had just been a helpless child, and it made their act sound far from gallant. Still somewhat in denial, they tried to defend themselves from the accusations, but Laura was on a roll.

"You're the ones who had better stay away from my library. I'd prefer a whole gang of thieves than pathetic bullies pretending to be heroes. Stupid, gutless morons, bullying little children."

It was a long time since Laura Libretto had got this mad with someone. She pointed at the road into town and suggested that the two thugs walked away from her, fast. Looking miserably at the ground as they put one foot in front of the other, still wondering what exactly had gone wrong in their glorious plan, they did as they were told.

23 DECEMBER – IF ONLY YOU READ THE CLASSICS

How stupid of me! I should have found the time. Anytime.

Laura had suffered a sleepless night. The thought that Jonas had tried to get to the library, even after the carabinieri's raid on his camp, filled her with pride for the little boy. But knowing that he'd had to cope with two idiots, three times his size, made her mad with anger.

I need to go and visit the Roma and explain what happened. I know a library isn't a school, I can't pretend it's ideal for the boy to be coming here to learn, but I simply can't sit by and do nothing.

At lunchtime, when she closed up after a special 'Christmas at the library' morning, she drove to the camp, half fearing she might find it empty. The caravans were still there, and so were the Roma, but no one approached her. They simply looked at her with icy glares.

"What more do you want from us?" a young woman asked finally when Laura made it obvious she had no intention of leaving.

"I'm here to speak to Maria, Jonas's grandmother," she replied.

The young woman disappeared towards the back of the

camp; the other Roma remained where they were, glaring at Laura. There was no curiosity in their eyes; this time, all she felt was a sense of open hostility.

Nonetheless, when the young woman reappeared, she asked the librarian to follow her. Before entering Maria's caravan, Laura felt like she was being watched, almost as if someone had been expecting her to show up. She turned and glimpsed Jonas, spying from behind the opening of a tent next to a caravan. He smiled at her and Laura was grateful for that smile; he knew she meant him no harm. They were still friends, despite the carabinieri's search, the accusations of narrow-minded people in the town, the bullying of the two jerks.

"Maria, here's the woman from the library, looking for you," the young woman called through the door. At least Laura was no longer being accused of being social services.

The door opened.

"Come in."

Laura sat exactly where she had sat the previous time. There was a certain weariness in the older woman's face.

"So, what do you want?"

"I know about the carabinieri search, and I'm very sorry. I don't believe any of you has anything to do with the thefts in town."

"We have got nothing to do with any crime. We're an honest bunch of people; none of my group has ever been in trouble with the police or carabinieri. And they know it!"

"As I said, I'm very sorry. And Jonas has stopped coming to the library, but I want him to know he is still welcome, anytime. I just wanted you to know that too."

"I'm not sure it's a good thing for him to go into that place at all. That's why I told him to stay away from town. When people start to think we're a threat to them, they become a threat to us. We are thinking of leaving the area instead of spending the winter here. Things will only get worse for us. So you see why it is hard for our kids to attend school. They can't drop in and out of classes; you'd never think that proper for your own kids."

"I was hoping you'd stay," said Laura. "But wherever you go, there will be a library, and it would be nice for Jonas to be able to attend. If you let me know where you are, I can get in touch with the librarian and ask them to provide him with a library card."

"Books fill his head with ideas that are too far from what he is and what he can do with his life."

"I was thinking of asking the librarians wherever you move to help Jonas, and the other kids if they're willing, with their preparation for school exams. He doesn't have to attend school, but he could be schooled in the libraries and take his exams each year."

"What for? To sell iron or beg in the streets?"

"You never know. There are scholarships for deserving students, but he needs to have the basics."

"You don't mean he can graduate, do you?" The woman was sceptical and taken aback at the same time.

"Why not? But to have a chance in the future, he needs to do something now. And wouldn't it be good to have someone who knows how to reply to the police, someone who knows about your rights? This is also what books can do for him."

"We can't control the future, nor things outside our camp."

"That's correct," said Laura, nodding. "There are a lot of things beyond our control – that holds true for everyone. But we can control how we react to things. We still make decisions day by day. And whether we're aware of it or not, every single decision we make, every single reaction to events shapes our future."

The old woman stood silently for a while before replying. "Why have you taken such a fancy to Jonas?"

"Because in his eyes I recognised the same hunger for books, for reading, for knowledge... You see, in my family, women weren't supposed to study beyond high school. We were to get married and take care of our family. Education for women was seen as a waste of money, something only for rich people."

"And you convinced your parents otherwise?"

"Yes, and I had the support of one of my high school teachers. My husband died when I had two young kids to bring up, so it was a good thing I had a job and a little money to raise them properly."

For the first time, the old Romani woman looked at Laura as if she was a human being, as if she could relate to her. Struggling for a living was something that put them on the same level.

"Where are your kids now?"

"They have their own families: one lives in Milan, the other in Rome, but they're both coming home for New Year's Eve. We love our reunions at this time of year."

"My family is all around me, always."

"That's lovely, you stick together all the time."

"This is why I feared you were from social services, and then I was afraid you might suggest Jonas should attend a school somewhere far away from us..."

"Oh no, never," Laura almost shrieked in horror at the very idea. "He's too young, and I would never suggest he should be taken away from his family."

"I haven't asked you if you want a cup of tea..."

"The same delicious tea you offered me last time?"

"There's a cinnamon bark thrown in the mix now, as it's Christmas time."

"I would love to try it."

The old woman filled two cups with hot, steamy tea, took a tray of fritters from the side and sat down in front of Laura. As they talked companionably of families, of the tough and the fun times they'd had as mothers, they didn't see Jonas creeping in, sitting on a chair in a dark corner and listening to them with dreamy eyes.

~

"MY GOODNESS, I NEVER THOUGHT WORKING IN A SHOP COULD tire you this much," grumbled Giò to Agnese as they said goodbye to Anna and Betta and made their way home after closing the perfumery.

"Oh, Giò, thanks so much for all your help. You and Anna have been simply wonderful, and you managed Mrs Lavecchia beautifully. I'm always afraid I'm going to lose patience with her."

"She's a trying woman, I don't know how her husband puts up with her."

"He is such a positive, charming man, I've no idea how he can bear all that negativity and dissatisfaction."

"At times, I wonder if men don't prefer women who make their lives miserable," Giò said, thinking of her 10 years with Dorian Gravy, an impossible man. What if she had been less accommodating, or just as demanding as he had been? Would that have saved their relationship?

"I prefer you as you are," said Agnese, as if reading her sister's thoughts. Giò smiled as a chilly gust of wind from the north swiped away all her nostalgic thoughts and hurried them both towards their warm home. "With all your million faults, but they're funny faults," Agnese added with a chuckle.

They reached home, passing through the communal main door from one of Maratea's many little alleys that gave access to three independent flats. Tonight, the family would all have dinner together at Agnese's. As they entered the first-floor flat, a mixture of smells enveloped them, from cinnamon and apples to focaccia and vincotto.

"I thought Christmas Eve was tomorrow," Giò laughed.

"It's just a light dinner," said Auntie Adelina.

"Only soup tonight," Granny confirmed.

Lilia, Luca and Nando's faces turned towards them in horror. Granny pretended to address her sister.

"But whoever finishes the soup can have a few pumpkin fritters."

"I see," Auntie Adelina replied.

"I can't believe the table is already laid and the food is waiting for us," said Agnese with a grateful smile. She was tired and she appreciated all her family did to support her through the most happy but demanding time of the year for the perfumery.

As everyone sat, a tray of cheese crostini appeared on the table, and from the happy smiles of the young Fiorillos, you could see that the soup was *not* just a common soup after all.

"How is work going?" Auntie Adelina asked.

"I'm really happy. Despite all the eShops and products available on the web, it seems people still love to buy in traditional shops – luckily."

"How's Anna coping with the job? You've been working nonstop this week."

"She's such a cheerful soul, always willing to do more."

"And I can pass all the most difficult customers on to her," said Giò, grinning.

"Which means I'm much more relaxed than when I see Giò trying to cope with them," Agnese added as all the family members chuckled loudly. "My only regret for this Christmas is that I haven't been able to help Mariella."

"What about her?" asked Granny.

"Didn't I tell you that she lost her job with Mrs Lavecchia?"

"I heard that from someone at the market, but I didn't give it much thought."

"Well..." and Agnese explained everything that had happened to the poor girl.

"With all the house thefts, people are so suspicious that no one Agnese has spoken to is inclined to look favourably on Mariella, even if they need help at home," Giò concluded. "It doesn't matter how much Agnese vouches for her, no one will even recommend her to their friends or acquaintances."

"And who's working for Mrs Lavecchia now?" Granny asked.

Giò shrugged.

"A new girl, Roberta," said Agnese. "I think she comes from Bari and I've only heard wonderful things about her."

"Who's saying wonderful things about her?" Granny said, a shrewd flash in her eyes.

"Mrs Lavecchia. The girl is extremely good looking and I believe she has even managed to charm Mrs Lavecchia's two nasty teenagers."

"And who else has she worked for?"

"She's only recently arrived here in Maratea. But why all these questions?"

"You need to file her details, don't you?" Giò teased Granny. "She isn't in your PGFS yet..."

"What's the PGFS?" Lilia asked.

"The Proud Gossip Filing System," Giò replied, winking at her.

"Giò," said Granny patiently, "I wish you would understand the importance of knowing what sort of people come into our village."

"As long as we respect their desire to keep things to themselves if they want to."

"If they want to keep things to themselves, they'd be better off moving to a large city rather than a small town," Auntie Adelina replied, embracing her sister's cause.

"You're such a couple of old hags camouflaged as sweet nannies. I can hardly believe I'm having this conversation in the 21st century, and the worst part of it is that I'm related to you."

Lilia and Luca, their heads on their arms, were watching what was promising to become a nice sparring match. They thoroughly enjoyed it when Auntie Giò argued with Granny. For her part, Granny always remained peaceful and calm, which made Giò even more furious. But Agnese didn't want a dispute just before Christmas.

"If I'm not wrong, I smell some delicious cinnamon. I guess there's dessert coming."

"We've made some nice little strudels." Lilia jumped up to fetch them from the lukewarm oven. When she came back to serve them, she made sure everyone knew what a great help she'd been.

"She learns fast, this lassie," Auntie Adelina said, patting Lilia on the shoulder. "She'll end up being a great cook."

"And Auntie Giò will be the only woman in the family not even able to fry an egg," added Luca.

"I forgot how hard it is spending Christmas at home," Giò grumbled, looking up at the ceiling with her palms spread out at shoulder height, as if to ask for mercy for her mistakes. "I had almost fooled myself into believing we'd have a pleasant time."

"Isn't Mrs Orlando a good friend of Mrs Lavecchia's?" asked Granny, ignoring Giò.

"They are very good friends indeed. Their families often spend time together," answered Agnese.

"And aren't the De Fino and Agosto families also very friendly with the Lavecchias?"

"They all belong to the same rather snobbish but closely knit circle of people. Both families were playing Tombola with Mrs Lavecchia when they were robbed. But I can't see the point of your questions, as certain as I am that there is one."

Granny responded to Agnese with another question. "Isn't Mrs Lavecchia's one of the few rich families that hasn't been robbed so far?"

"Again, you're right. And again, I don't understand your point. Do you?" Agnese asked Nando and Giò. They both shrugged.

"What about you, Adele, can you see my point?" asked Granny.

"Of course I can. Mrs Lavecchia had better watch out for her family silver as soon as all her friends' homes have been emptied."

Now five faces were turned towards the two old women, watching them intently. Granny, who had enjoyed acting in her youth and still had a good sense of the dramatic, stayed silent for a little while. Just long enough to make her listeners even more desperate, if that were possible, for an explanation.

Finally, she gave in. "Ah! If you only read the classics."

Adelina nodded in approval.

"Classic what?" Giò asked.

"Classic mysteries. If you read the classics, then you'd know that the easiest way to commit a robbery is to get a job as a housekeeper or a nanny in a well-off home and study the habits of your employer's rich friends, getting to know the people who work for them. Then all you have to do is pass on information to the rest of the gang."

"It's that simple," Auntie Adelina added.

"You mean this Roberta is passing information to the thieves?"

"Why not?" Granny said, raising and dropping her shoulders. The adults' jaws almost fell to the table, while the children asked if Granny and Auntie Adelina had solved the case of the thefts.

"But how would she know that Mariella would be fired?" asked Agnese as soon as she could string the words together.

"Maybe she found a way to drop those earrings into her coat pocket?"

"I see," Agnese replied, still uncertain what to believe.

"We're going to have to find out if these two old hags may be right," said Giò, jumping up to fetch her mobile and ring Paolo. The call went straight to voicemail, so Giò left him a message to check who Roberta, Mrs Lavecchia's latest housekeeper, was and if she could, by any chance, be involved in the robberies.

"And until we know for sure, all of this has to be kept quiet," said Nando, the first one to swear on his honour to protect the secret or he wouldn't eat a sweet for the whole of the Christmas season. His children then swore solemnly to do the same.

24 DECEMBER – A JOURNEY THROUGH
THE SNOW

I t was 8.30am when Paolo rang Giò.

"You were quick, I only messaged you twelve hours ago."

"I wanted to tell you that you might be right. But how did you know?"

"Know what?"

"That Roberta Taralli has a rather interesting past. She is not on the official records – apparently she's never committed a crime, but a few phone calls to the carabinieri in Bari made some things crystal clear. It seems wherever Roberta Taralli has gone, trouble has always followed. Never for the family she worked for, but all their rich friends have been the victims of well-planned robberies. They suspect she passes information on to her husband and brother, telling them exactly what they will find and where."

"My goodness, the two hags were right! I can't believe it."

"Giò, what did you just mumble about two eggs? I didn't catch a single word…"

"Don't you worry about that. What are you going to do now?"

"Very little, I'm afraid. It looks as though the gang of thieves is one step ahead of us. Last night, Roberta Taralli told a broken-hearted Mrs Lavecchia that she was going to have to leave. Her dear aunt in Bari isn't feeling well, apparently, and she's had to go back to look after her. She left early this morning."

"So three criminals are going to celebrate a very merry Christmas?"

"Don't you worry, from now on, they will be followed wherever they go. It's only a matter of time before we catch them. They'd better enjoy their Christmas, because by New Year they will be in jail. But how did *you* know?"

"It's a long story that I will tell you in detail some other time. For now, let me remind you how important it is to read the classics."

"What classics?"

"Mysteries."

Paolo gulped, momentarily wrong-footed, but was soon ready with his next question. "How about your parcel?"

"I've just tracked my parcel. It's in transit, but I'll keep calling to make sure the delivery is today."

IT WASN'T MUCH LATER THAT PAOLO TOOK A CALL ON HIS MOBILE phone. It was Giò ringing him this time, updating him in her most frantic voice.

"Paolo, I tracked our parcel. It will get to Lauria at lunchtime, but they won't do deliveries this afternoon as the weather is so bad. Heavy snowstorms are sweeping the area, so they will only deliver to the nearest towns, and even that may not be possible. So I'm going to drive to Lauria to fetch it."

"Aren't you working at your sister's perfumery?"

"She said she and Anna can manage without me."

"But you've not got winter tyres on your car."

"No, I don't," Giò admitted in despair, thinking of her sister's tiny old car. It wasn't built for driving in the snow.

"I'm on duty till 6pm. Which courier firm have you used?"

"Fast & Furious Parcels Ltd."

"And they sent the parcel in your name, didn't they?"

"Exactly."

"Give me 10 minutes, I'll call you back."

Paolo actually called after three minutes. "One of the Fast & Furious chaps in Lauria is a very good friend of mine. He is taking the parcel home with him. Be at the carabinieri station at ten to six, we won't have much time."

"It will be snowing hard on the mountains."

"And you'll have one heck of a good driver!"

AT HALF PAST FIVE, GIÒ ARRIVED AT THE CARABINIERI STATION IN Fiumicello. The rain was falling in buckets from the sky, so she didn't dare get out of the car, but that was more because she'd rather avoid Maresciallo Mangiaboschi than the weather. This arrogant man had on a number of occasions made it clear they would never get on well. She didn't want to test their relationship just before Christmas.

It was five minutes to six when Paolo called her, and by six o'clock, his car was beside hers. She jumped out of her driver's seat straight into his car.

Normally, it would have taken around 40 minutes to cover the 30 kilometres to Lauria, but today the rain was rattling furiously against the car. The windscreen wipers were at full speed, but still the two passengers could hardly see more than a few metres ahead. Slowly, slowly, bend after bend, they climbed to Trecchina, a mere 10 kilometres from Maratea. Would they ever get to Lauria?

By the time they reached the Statale 585, the rain had turned solid. The road was already completely white and the cars were proceeding with great difficulty. Visibility was virtually zero and the road surface was treacherous and slippery. Paolo had to open the window from time to time to remove the piles of snow, turning rapidly to ice, that had accumulated on the sides of the windscreen, packed in tightly by the windscreen wipers and further obstructing the view. Each time, he would shake his hand, grimacing in pain from the touch of the snow and the furious wind freezing it. And they were proceeding at what? Ten kilometres per hour?

"What now?" gasped Giò when the intensifying storm brought the line of cars in front of them to a halt. Paolo, for once, didn't have an answer.

Ten minutes later, the cars had their hazard lights on and no one was moving forward. They saw people venturing out of the cars, standing upright with difficulty under the force of the strong gusts of wind.

"Wait for me here," said Paolo.

"Where are you going?"

"I need to know what's happening."

"We've stopped because of the snow, isn't that clear enough?" Giò cried, thinking gloomily that after years away from home, she would end up spending her first Christmas Eve back in Maratea sitting in a car with a local carabiniere.

Undeterred, Paolo left, and Giò looked on in horror at how much more snow was falling on the road. Darkness didn't allow her line of vision to wander very far, but everything that was illuminated by the car headlights was covered with snow. It was as if the whole world had been drained of colour.

And from the shadows of the colourless world, a shivering

snowman wobbled up to the car and asked to be allowed back in. As Giò pushed the door open for him, Paolo got inside, breathing onto his hands to try and restore some feeling to them. Giò pulled his frozen purple fingers into her hands and massaged them with vigour and an unexpected dose of affection. Nonetheless, it took a good couple of minutes before Paolo could unseal his lips.

"A truck has slipped on the ice, blocking the road in both directions. We need to wait for the emergency services…"

"Can't we go back and find an alternative route?"

Paolo didn't answer, just pointed to the long queue of cars behind them, reflected in the rear-view mirror.

"Oh my goodness, we're really stuck!"

The snow kept falling, indifferent to Giò's dismay and her ruined Christmas plans. It was almost eight o'clock before Paolo finally cried, "They're coming!" Looking in the rear-view mirror, he had spotted the blue lights of the emergency services, snowplough included.

It took 20 minutes before the long line of cars could get started again and slowly follow the snowplough-cleared track. It was almost nine o'clock when Paolo pulled up outside his courier friend's home, getting the precious parcel, together with the good news that the snowstorm was easing. It looked as though they would make it back home much more easily than their journey out had been, but they still had to drive extremely slowly. The wind was dying down, but big snowflakes were dancing softly in the air.

"Are you going to open it?" Paolo asked Giò, who kept fiddling with the parcel.

"I have to."

With trembling hands, she tore the plastic bag open, and there it was: the white envelope containing the DNA test results. She opened it. Switching on the car's interior light, she extracted the results and read them out loud.

"The two DNA profiles are compatible. There's a 90% probability they are related."

Giò clapped her hands and hugged Paolo's free arm. They cheered, they hurrahed, and then Paolo had to go back to being extra careful while driving. The snow was deep in some places and starting to freeze in others, but at least the traffic had disappeared.

Her phone rang. "Where are you?" Agnese asked. "We've not started dinner yet; we're waiting for you."

"We're on our way, and with plenty of good news. Please prepare a nice gift box. This is one Christmas present I want to wrap extra nicely."

AFTER AN ABUNDANT IF RATHER LATE DINNER, GIÒ AND HER family exchanged presents with Anna, Betta and Mrs De Blasi at midnight. It had never happened before, but even Luca and Lilia were postponing opening their presents, waiting with impatience to see what would happen next. All eyes were on Mrs De Blasi as she looked at the small blue Tiffany box in her hands, tied beautifully with a white ribbon, and read the card out loud.

"To Mrs De Blasi, and Anna and Betta." The elderly woman raised her head, confused. "For the three of us?" she asked, looking at Giò, and then Agnese.

"Yes, for the three of you. From all of us."

"Betta, do you want to open it?"

Of course, Betta could not wait. She opened the box, found the white envelope and read aloud, "DNA Track Company."

"Is it about your research, Giò?" Anna asked.

"Yes and no. It's more about your family."

Betta read the contents of the letter. The two women seemed literally frozen and uncertain what to think.

"Giò has done lots of research on your behalf," Agnese explained. "She couldn't understand the striking similarity between Betta and Marco; the fact your Alex had a postcard of Maratea, Anna; that Alex used to sing the same tune Marco's grandmother's carillon plays. Eventually, she started to think that Alex and Marco could be the same person."

"But Marco passed away in 2005, before Betta was born," stuttered Mrs De Blasi.

"I believe it was actually a man called Davide Bortolin who passed away then," Giò said, "a poor young vagrant. You mentioned your husband going to Milan to identify the body, Mrs De Blasi. Did he tell you what he saw?"

"He said my son was badly burned, but he recognised what was left. Also, the authorities found a partly burned ID and Marco's personal belongings. We were left in no doubt it was him."

"I believe Marco had been there and tried to help Bortolin escape from the fire. But when he realised he could do nothing to save the man's life, he wondered if he could turn the tragedy into an opportunity to break free from his past and make sure, once and for all, that his father couldn't track him. I believe Marco assumed Davide Bortolin's identity."

"But what's this got to do with Alex?" Anna asked.

"Marco soon found that although his new identity sheltered him from his father, it was a heavy burden to carry around. Bortolin had certainly had a tough past, including prison and drugs, so Marco made up his mind two years later to apply for a new identity. He hadn't been able to ask for one to get away from a cruel father, but as Bortolin, he could. Maybe he told the authorities his past could put him in danger – I don't know. But he could prove that in the past two years, he – or rather, Davide Bortolin – had become a reliable fellow. The judges accorded him a new identity, and in 2007, Marco became Alex."

Giò looked at Anna. The woman's eyes were fixed on her, her expression unreadable.

"This is why it was so difficult to dig into Alex's past. I had to ask for help from the carabinieri, but neither I nor they could find anything about Alex Giordano that was dated before 2007. Then Paolo – a carabinieri brigadiere and friend – suggested it might be the case that he was someone who had applied for a new identity."

There was a long pause. Mrs De Blasi had gone pale and her hands were trembling. Finally, Anna spoke.

"I'm not sure I'm following everything you're saying, Giò. But did you say the vagrant – Bortolin?" Giò nodded. "Did you say Bortolin died in a fire?"

"Yes."

"It was one of Alex's recurring nightmares, a hovel on fire." Anna gulped. "He told me that he had tried to save a young man from a fire, but when he got to him, it was too late."

"My goodness," Mrs De Blasi whispered.

Agnese said softly, "I'm sure that if you keep talking, the two of you will find more and more things in common."

Anna took the piece of paper from her daughter's hands and reread it over and over again.

"Here it says there's a 90% *probability* Betta and Mrs De Blasi are related. What does it mean?"

"The test between a grandmother and granddaughter isn't 100% conclusive," Giò said. "There was a risk the two profiles could have turned out to be very different, even if they were related. But in your case, they didn't. Of course, you're likely to want to run other tests in the future. But I feel confident that Mrs De Blasi and Betta are related."

To Giò's great dismay, the atmosphere was heavy and awkward. The two women stayed stock-still and made no attempt to look at each other. Betta stared at her mother, not too sure what was going on. She had a feeling it was good news, but the expression on her mother's face told her otherwise.

Giò had expected a burst of joy, Agnese thought, looking at her sister's disappointed face. *And now she looks so crestfallen by their reaction. But we should have guessed. It's overwhelming for both Anna and Mrs De Blasi, and they must fear this whole affair might just end up like a bubble, bursting into thin air and leading to harsh disappointment later.*

"Well, I'd say there's been enough talking. Let's open all the presents," Nando said merrily. It was a good way to alleviate the embarrassment.

Lilia and Luca distributed all the presents, and finally there was laughter and a few hugs, at least on the part of the Fiorillos and Brandos. Then Mrs De Blasi called Betta over. The child had just opened her mum's present.

"What do you have around your neck?"

"This is my present from Mum, now that I'm grown up," Betta said, showing the elderly woman a necklace holding a silver medallion.

Mrs De Blasi looked shocked for the second time that night. "I know what that is. There's a name on the back of the medallion, isn't there?"

"It's my own name," Betta said, turning her charm round. "Well, almost. It says 'Elisabeth'."

"And a date of birth – 5-5-1932."

"How did you know?" asked Betta in wonder.

"That was my mother-in-law's medallion," said Mrs De Blasi. "She gave it to my son to pass on to his children."

"This is the only family heirloom my husband left me," Anna cried in wonder.

"Marco loved his Scottish grandma so much."

Betta looked at the two women. "Does this mean you are *my* grandma, Mrs De Blasi?"

"I'd say I am," replied Mrs De Blasi, tears in her eyes. "Though I'm not sure I deserve the title after the way I treated your father…"

But before she could say another word, the little girl with the green eyes, so strikingly similar to those of Mrs De Blasi's son, and her mother both threw themselves into the old woman's arms. Finally, Giò had the happy Christmas she had hoped for.

25 DECEMBER – A FAMILY CHRISTMAS

I t was an extraordinarily merry Christmas for the Brandos. After years apart, they finally managed to get together for the festivities. When Agnese headed for her bedroom in the evening, she was more than a little tired, but blissfully happy.

As was her habit whenever life threw up something remarkable, she made a special note in her diary – a simple bullet list to help her remember and learn from life's at times bizarre lessons.

- What a strange coincidence that Anna and Betta should have come here, to Maratea. That the robin – or perhaps a ghost from the past speaking through him – should have said the word *carillon* and set Giò going. Granny claims it's an ancient tradition that animals can speak to humans, but that's meant to be on Christmas night, not on the second of December!
- Poor Giò and Paolo! Their rush through the snow proved pointless once we discovered that Anna had the medallion that had belonged to Elisabeth,

Betta's great-grandmother, all along. Let's just say that the news she returned with set the scene for the story to unfold.

- Anna and Betta will no longer have to fear for their future; Mrs De Blasi has already said that her son's inheritance will go to them straight away. I believe they will end up living in Maratea, especially if Anna manages to find a job, or perhaps start her own business.

- Anna has told the Pink Slippers Society that the money they had been collecting for her can now go to some other worthy cause, and she's suggested they could use it to help Jonas finance his studies. Mrs Capello has agreed to contact other Pink Slippers societies in Italy after Christmas, suggesting they assist him and all the kids in his community by finding volunteers to teach them in libraries wherever they go. By the end of the school year, they will be ready to take their first school exams.

- I know it's an un-Christmassy thing to say, but I can't wait for Maratea to discover who the real thieves were. If Mrs Lavecchia had just trusted her original housekeeper, Mariella, then a lot of thefts could have been avoided. After this, I'm certain Mariella will be able to pick and choose the family she wants to work for…

- But there are even more twists to come. Paolo asked Strazio, his subordinate, to have a friendly word with Mrs Lavecchia's sons. They play football with Strazio's own teenage son, and the team and their parents got together this morning to exchange Christmas greetings. Apparently, Strazio's manner is so easy going that… the two ~~devils~~ boys felt

relaxed enough to confess they were the ones who
had planted the diamond earrings in Mariella's
coat. They admitted that they'd first met Roberta
Taralli back in November – she *just happened* to be
hanging around the school – and were so taken by
her charms, they were amenable to the *subtle*
suggestion they get rid of their mother's current
and rather unattractive housekeeper. So as soon as
they could, they dropped the two earrings into the
poor girl's pocket.

- As usual, rather than reproaching her sons, Mrs
Lavecchia tried to defend them, saying they only
planted the earrings as a joke. She also maintains –
and this is true – that they never thought the
charming Roberta had anything to do with the
thefts. Despite this, Mr Lavecchia has decided to
punish the two spoiled brats, this very afternoon
asking the mayor to make them work over the
Christmas holidays to keep the town clean. They
will join the two bullies who threatened Jonas. It
was Laura Libretto who suggested that if they
really wanted to help make Maratea a better place,
they'd better start with a broomstick.

- And… I shouldn't really say it, but I feel such
satisfaction regarding Mrs Lavecchia. I'm sure all
this will do her some good. Now I've written it
down, I feel so much better and can get back to
enjoying our splendid Christmas.

- Talking of which, Granny and Auntie Adelina
didn't have one single fight during the meal
preparations. Valerio and his family really did come
over and will stay for a couple more days so that
Giorgia and Lilia, Luca and Giacomo can spend a
lovely time together.

- Emmegra – dear Emmegra – has changed quite a lot since last year. She's become so sweet, particularly towards Granny and Auntie Adelina. It has been a truly old-fashioned family Christmas, all together again, having a huge party. It's lovely that all the members of the family should get along this well. That's the true spirit of Christmas.

THE END

DEAR READER,

I hope you enjoyed this novella. There are three more books available featuring Giò Brando, and new ones to come.

In the meantime…

Is there any way a reader may help an author? Yes! Please leave a review on **your favourite e-store, Goodreads** and/or **Bookbub**. It doesn't matter how long or short it is; even a single sentence can say all that needs to be said. We may live in a digital era, but **this old world of ours still revolves around word of mouth**. A review allows a book to leave the shadows of the unknown and introduces it to other passionate readers.

GRAZIE :)

GLOSSARY

APERITIVO – this is a convivial social event, often in a bar with friends before heading home for the family lunch or dinner. Let's say it's a sort of appetiser before the real meal. It can be simple or lavish, merely a drink or a variety of finger food. In Italy, we also invite people home for an aperitivo, which is not as formal as a proper meal, but beware! Like Granny's panzerotti, it can be delicious, moreish and *very* filling.

BRIGADIERE – **plural brigadieri:** this can be loosely compared to a detective sergeant. In the carabinieri ranks, a brigadiere operates below a maresciallo.

CARABINIERE – **plural carabinieri:** in Italy, we don't only have the polizia (much like the police in most countries), we also have the carabinieri. Essentially, this is another police force, but it's part of the army and is governed by the Ministry of Defence, whereas the polizia depends on the Ministry of the Interior.

Being part of the military, the carabinieri tend to wear

their uniforms more than the polizia, even when investigating crimes. The two are often in competition (though they won't admit it), so never confuse one with the other (especially if you're talking with Maresciallo Mangiaboschi, he is rather touchy). For me, the only difference between the two is that we Italians have a number of cracking jokes about the carabinieri and none about the polizia. Don't ask me why.

In Maratea, there's only the carabinieri and no polizia. But Paolo would have been a carabiniere and not a policeman in any case.

CARILLON – it's a musical box. Because of its French sound, I thought it was a sort of 'international' word, but when my editor wrote back to me, asking me what it meant, I realised I was wrong. Apparently, we Italians adapted it from the French *quarregnon* or *carignon*, referring to the sound of bells singing a melody.

Also, the pronunciation is misleading, since a double L in Italian is pronounced as a slightly emphasised L (as in tarantella), but we pronounce this word in the Spanish way. It is a rather uncommon sound in English, like a stronger Y.

As a kid, I had a fascination with carillons of all kinds. I thought they were rare, precious objects, mainly belonging to grannies who used them to store their jewels. To be allowed to play with one of those boxes was a special prize indeed.

CARTELLATE – I have mixed things up in the story. Cartellate are a traditional Christmas sweet mainly from Apulia rather than Maratea, but I guess Granny's family, very much like my own, may originate from there. They are a sort of fritter, but they are thin and give a delightful crunch before melting in your mouth.

As you saw with Granny and Auntie Adelina, there are

endless debates as to the best recipe for cartellate and whether they should be coated in must or fig vincotto, or honey.

CRODINO – a popular non-alcoholic soda used in Italy for the aperitivo.

MARESCIALLO – this rank is similar to detective inspector. A maresciallo is superior to a brigadiere, carabiniere semplice and appuntato.

PANZEROTTO – **plural panzerotti:** small calzone made with the same dough as pizza, filled with mozzarella, tomato and fresh basil leaves, and deep fried. Want to know more about them? Read Book 1, *Murder on the Road*.

SALUTE! – **or CIN CIN** (pronounced chin chin): this is the equivalent of 'Cheers!' When celebrating an event with a glass of wine or prosecco, we love to accompany the word by clinking our glasses together.

TOMBOLA and MERCANTE IN FIERA are two popular Christmas games. The first one is similar to Bingo, the second one is a card game played by large groups of people.

If you have found other Italian words in the story and would like to know what they mean, please let me know.

Contact me on:
Twitter: @adrianalici
Join the Maratea Murder Club

JOIN THE MARATEA MURDER CLUB

You'll get exclusive content:

- **Book 0,** *And Then There Were Bones,* the prequel to the *An Italian Village Mystery* series available nowhere else
- **Giò Brando's Maratea Album** – photos of her favourite places and behind-the-scenes secrets
- **A Maratea Map** – including most places featured in the series
- **Adriana Licio's News** – new releases, news from Maratea, but no spam – Giò would loathe it!
- **Cosy Mystery Passion:** a place to share favourite books, characters, tips and tropes

Join here – it's free:
www.adrianalicio.com/murderclub

MORE BOOKS FROM ADRIANA LICIO

And Then There Were Bones, prequel to the *An Italian Village Mystery* series, is only available by signing up to **www.adrianalicio.com/murderclub** You can unsubscribe any time you like, but of course, I hope you will stay.

Murder on the Road is the first book in the series, and it lets you know how and why Giò Brando decided to come back to Maratea (and what else life has in store for her).

A Fair Time for Death is a mystery set during the Autumn Chestnut Fair in Trecchina, a mountain village near Maratea, involving a perfume with a split personality, a disappearing corpse, a disturbing secret from the past and a mischievous goat.

The fourth book in the series is in progress and should reach you around springtime 2020. Wish me luck with the Muse!

ABOUT THE AUTHOR

Adriana Licio lives in the Apennine Mountains in southern Italy, not far from Maratea, the seaside setting for her first cosy series, *An Italian Village Mystery*. Adriana returns to Maratea looking for peace and quiet, but inevitably stumbles on beguiling places and intriguing stories every time. She says time for relaxing will come – sooner or later.

She loves loads of things: travelling, reading, walking, sgood food, small villages, and home swapping. A long time ago, she spent six years falling in love with Scotland, and she has never recovered. She now runs her family perfumery, and between a dark patchouli and a musky rose, she devours cosy mysteries.

She resisted writing as long as she could, fearing she might get carried away by her fertile imagination. But one day, she found an alluring blank page and the words flowed in the weird English she'd learned in Glasgow.

Adriana finds peace for her restless, enthusiastic soul by walking in nature with her adventurous golden retriever Frodo and her hubby Giovanni.

Do you want to know more?
Join the **Maratea Murder Club**

You can also stay in touch on:
www.adrianalicio.com

facebook.com/adrianalicio.mystery

twitter.com/adrianalici

amazon.com/author/adrianalicio

bookbub.com/profile/adriana-licio

AUTHOR'S NOTE

I'm very sorry if I may disappoint any of you, but I have to confess I've never spent Christmas in Maratea. It's a rather hectic time for my business, so I've never gone anywhere during the Christmas season.

And it's always been like that since I was a kid. My mum owned a perfumery, and the whole month of December was dedicated to working in the business. But at 8pm on 24 December, we'd close the shop and have a long drive, often through the snow, all the way to Bari where the rest of the family – including five sisters and our grandparents – were patiently waiting for our homecoming before starting dinner. I loved the whole occasion – the exciting trip with the snow coming down, the huge dinner and, of course, the anticipation of waiting for Santa to come…

As for Maratea, it is such a small place that, despite what Mayor Zucchini may say, I suspect not many tourists visit at Christmas, so the decorations may not be quite as rich as I described. I'm not sure the townsfolk hold a Christmas Market, either, but they should, shouldn't they? Still, I'd love to be able to spend at least one Christmas there. In the meantime, I decided I'd describe a Christmas in Maratea exactly as I imagine it to be, and the Brandos were kind enough to give me permission.

In 2017, Maratea was chosen to host the New Year's Eve concert for RAI 1, Italy's national TV station. Again, I was not able to attend, but I watched it on the screen. It was fascinating, and those images have definitely contributed to getting this story going.

My valiant editor, who often acts as a cultural interpreter, has suggested that I add a final note regarding school hours and shop opening and closing times in Maratea for people not familiar with Southern Italy. Primary schools will, for the most part, be open six days a week from 8.30am to 1.30pm, and children get back home in time to have lunch with their families at around 2pm. Mostly they don't go back to school in the afternoons, except for those doing extracurricular activities. In small towns such as Maratea, these are rare.

Shop opening times may sound even stranger: 9am to 1.30pm, and then 5 to 8.30pm. Most shops will be closed on Sundays except in high summer (for places near the sea) and at Christmastime, when they might open earlier in the afternoon and close later. There are likely to be differences from region to region, and town to town.

If you walk into a restaurant at six or seven in the evening, unless you're in a location that attracts international tourists, you'll either find it's closed or the waiters will give you a funny look. In Italy, we don't tend to eat before 8pm, and if you run a small independent shop, as Agnese and I do, you're likely to have dinner at 9pm or later.

So if you travel down south – maybe to visit Maratea – be ready to embrace a time-travel adventure.

I regularly share photos of the places I use in my books on Facebook, so you might want to give them a look here: www.facebook.com/adrianalicio.mystery

Made in the USA
Columbia, SC
10 November 2020